CARLY REID

Death in Dalkinchie

Dalkinchie Mysteries Book 1

D1466647

Inkpot Books

This book was professionally typeset on Reedsy.
Find out more at reedsy.com

Contents

1

Reporting for Duty

"Remind me of your plans today, Jessica?"

Reenie Maguire ran her hand distractedly through her mop of auburn curls, held back with her customary blue bandana. She sat at the scrubbed wooden dining table in her cozy little cottage, in the village of Dalkinchie in Perthshire, Scotland. With her other hand she held the remnants of a soft squeaky toy fox, currently being enthusiastically worried by a young tan and white puppy with soft, floppy ears. Opposite sat Reenie's niece Jessica Greer, a young woman in her 20s. Between them lay the remnants of their breakfast, but both women were still enjoying large mugs of tea – the first of many, as Jessica was becoming accustomed to after eight weeks in Scotland.

"I'm reporting on the Dalkinchie Craft Show! I'm sure I have mentioned it once or twice over the last couple of weeks." Jessica teased her aunt.

"No, I remember that, of course. I was wondering what your timings were. Whether there was any wee break in the day for you to take little miss Willow here for a walk with me."

Willow tugged away at the ragged toy, her eyes fixed on Reenie. Even at this early stage, her ears flickered slightly at the word "walk" and definitely turned upwards at the sound of her name. Jessica observed this, smiling at the pup's antics as she finally bested Reenie and settled down with the toy fox between her paws, chewing determinedly on its knotted tail.

"Well, Grant wants me to observe the whole process, from the checking in of items through set up and judging, and then later on this evening the award ceremony. There will be a gap between registration and judging, and then judging and the show opening, but I think I'll work in the newspaper offices – there's a lot to write and a tight turnaround to get it in next week's paper.

"Tomorrow the hall stays open and people can put up items for sale. The report will mostly be about the show, atmosphere and ambience and so on, and then an exhaustive list of all the winners, but he thinks I will be better able to understand how it all fits together if I observe from the start. He's probably right. I think it's quite a big deal," Jessica finished, remembering conversations she had had with villagers over the past week, including her friend Ealisaid Robertson who owned and ran *Lissa's,* the local café and coffee shop.

"So I hear," remarked Reenie. She ran her own business, The Bloom Room, a small flower shop in Dalkinchie, but it was a recent enterprise and a big shift from her previous career as a corporate event florist in Edinburgh. Neither of them had yet witnessed a full yearly cycle in Dalkinchie, and it was the first Craft Show weekend for both of them. As she spoke, Willow discarded her toy and jumped up, barrelling over to Reenie and pawing at her knee. "Woof!"

Reenie reached into the pocket of her zipped fleece top and

produced some small treats. She held the treat in the air, just above the puppy's nose. "Willow, sit!"

Immediately Willow sat obediently, her eyes fixed on the treat which she soon received, along with a "Good dog!"

"So, I think there will be some coming and going, but I will be at the Village Hall for a lot of the day. I'll try to pop in, but I also have to try and dodge Nicholas Pringle who is still after me about last week's local community group meeting. I think he wants to have his say in what I'll report, but I've already nearly finished it. Do you have a busy day in the shop?"

Reenie was only half paying attention, trying to get Willow to lie down for her treat. Failing to do so, she accomplished another successful 'sit!' command and followed up by placing a treat on the ground a few feet from the puppy and saying 'stay!' This was a miserable failure. Willow seemed to have no concept of waiting for her treat and scurried over as soon as the treat touched the floor. She'd gobbled it up before Reenie could remove it.

"Sorry, Jessica, what was it you said?"

"I just asked if you would be busy today."

"Nicely busy. I have a couple of arrangements to be picked up, a few orders for gifts, and someone coming in to talk about flowers for a silver wedding in the afternoon. Plus the usual walk-ins, and perhaps there will be more of those if the village is busy for the Show."

Reenie stood up, and looked towards the window.

"It's looking like a lovely day and it would be nice if there were more visitors from out of town, happy to spread the word about the new, charming flower shop! I was wondering if you'd be able to join me for lunch and a walk, but it doesn't sound likely. I won't make it to the Show, although I might pop along tomorrow. I could make you a sandwich, and I was thinking of just picking up some fish and chips for dinner, would that suit you? You might be glad of it after a long day."

"I'd like that, but I keep telling you Reenie, you don't have to look after me. I can sort out my own lunch and dinner on days like this."

Jessica had joined her aunt in Scotland earlier in the summer after a bad breakup with her long-term boyfriend had forced her to re-evaluate her post-college summer plans – and in fact, her entire life plans. Leaving her family and her secured place at journalism grad school in the U.S.A, she had committed to living in Scotland for a least a year, working as a part-time reporter for *The Dalkinchie & Drummond Herald* under the supervision of its editor, Grant Mack, and also working occasional shifts when either her aunt or Ealisaid needed another member of staff. This plan had so far worked extremely well, and Jessica found she enjoyed living with her aunt very much. Reenie and Jessica's mom Bella were twins, and although outwardly quite different – Bella was a lawyer, and had the professional demeanour to match – their closeness meant that Jessica felt entirely comfortable as a member of Reenie's household. Plus, here she didn't have to fight over the shower with her siblings, her two younger twin sisters Kyla and Lorna, and the baby of the family, their brother Alexander.

Her mom's Scottish upbringing meant that Jessica hadn't experienced too much of a culture shock, having visited Reenie in Edinburgh many times and even traveled around a little in the past. However, she was still learning every day – not just about life in Scotland, but about living in a close-knit village community. Having everyone know your business definitely took some getting used to. And now they had thrown dog-training into the mix as well. Reenie had planned to get a dog at some point after she moved to Dalkinchie, but events were precipitated when a springer spaniel puppy became available in a local litter. One look, and both Reenie and Jessica had been completely smitten. Willow was now a part of their family, and they were attempting to train her on some basic commands, with only mixed success. Although she had nailed 'sit' she had always struggled with 'stay', and as for 'down' - forget it!

"Och, I enjoy it, you know I do. Fish & chips it is then. I'll pick them up after closing and I'll keep yours warm in the oven. You can text if you are going to be very late."

"Sure. I had better head off now. I want to be there for the jam and preserves registration, because Ealisaid is booking that one in and I know she'll be patient about explaining the process to me. It seems extremely complicated!" said Jessica, thinking of the forms she had already seen, and the printed list of proceedings she had in her folder.

"Jams and preserves? Oh, maybe I'll enter. I'm quite proud of my latest batch of blaeberry and bramble jam. Would you be able to take a jar up for me?" Although Reenie was addressing Jessica, she was distracted by the dog who had now curled up on her feet and closed her eyes.

"Too late Reenie! Registration for entrants closed two weeks ago. It's just admittance that's happening today, and you would need to already have an entrant number. I did give you the form..."

"Oh of course you did, I remember. Not to worry, there's always next year. You can scope out the competition for me. Tell me who the real threats are! Anyway, I hope you have a good day. This is an exciting assignment Grant has given you. It's a really popular show, and I'm sure you will learn a lot."

5

"Thanks. I am excited. Grant says that he usually gives events like this four pages – including the centre double-page spread. That's the most I'll have written for the paper so far, but I'm sure I can do it, and it will be interesting to learn more about traditional Scottish crafts in the process."

"I'll see you when I see you, then. Enjoy it, and I hope there's no controversy at the judging!"

Reenie was making a joke, but she couldn't have known how prophetic her words would turn out to be.

* * *

The hustle and bustle was already evident by the time that Jessica got to the Village Hall. The normally sparsely-filled car park was completely full, and people were carefully making their way across the street into the large weathered stone building, ferrying bundles of textiles and carved wooden items such as chairs, footstools and small tables.

She knew that the show was divided into different classes by types of craft, and then within those classes there were subdivisions called categories. You could enter as many different classes as you wanted, but a maximum of three categories per class. At least, she thought that was the case. It might be an idea to check again.

Entrants were able to bring their goods to the show and officially register them on the morning of the Show, with half an hour allocated to this process per class. Once this was achieved, entrants were able to set up their crafts on the designated tables in the large hall, where they would then have to leave them for the judging to take place. By 11 o'clock, Jessica had been told, everyone would have left the Village

Hall apart from the various sets of judges, who would move around, making notes, conferring and finally appointing the first, second and third prizes and marking them with coloured dots which would then be replaced by beautifully penned cards. Grant had secured permission for Jessica to be present in the hall at this point in order to make her notes with a clear view of all the exhibits without any people in the way. The same privilege had been bestowed upon Magnus Smith, a sometime freelance photographer for *The D&D Herald*, as it was known locally.

Jessica couldn't deny that this was a pleasing turn of events. She had met the part-time farmer, part-time photographer socially as well as working with him a couple of times, and found him relaxed and easy-going company.

From 2.30pm to 5pm the Show would reopen to entrants, and to the general public as well. At 6pm there was an award ceremony, with several cups and trophies available for excellence in particular classes. Jessica looked forward to hearing the history of these, some of which had been donated by local organisations, and others set up in memory of village personalities. For now, however, she headed straight for one of the smaller side halls held within the building, where she knew Ealisaid was tasked with registering entries in all the categories within both the jams and preserves, and the cakes classes.

"Morning, Jessica!"

Ealisaid sat behind a small desk just inside the door, ticking people and entries off on a clipboard and directing them towards the correct section of the tables which were set up on three sides of the room. One was already covered with an assortment of cakes, while the one on the opposite wall under the window was beginning to fill up with jewel-colored jars, and the table at the back was bare save for a draped snowy-white tablecloth. Three chairs were evenly placed behind it. The judging table. Ealisaid had already explained that the edible classes were judged separately from the rest of the crafts, requiring tasting and independent verification by a panel of three, of which she was one.

Jessica was used to seeing her friend dealing with a line of people. Ealisaid had been the sole proprietor and manager of her café for nearly ten years, since she was 19. The two women had become friends immediately after Jessica arrived in Dalkinchie, and although Ealisaid did not have much free time, had got closer in the intervening months. Now Jessica was glad to see her, knowing that at least one person would be patient and happy to answer any questions she had.

She had not heard the same about the head judge and show convenor, Desmond Wilcott, who was reputed to be quite unbending and humorless, and was responsible for many of the rules and regulations that defined the day. Still, looking around, Jessica could appreciate the need for them. Everything was running in an orderly and logical fashion. Signs on the walls clearly laid out the timescales for the day and informed entrants of what they would need to bring. Signs beside the individual tables laid out the requirements for the classes, and Jessica knew that these were a repeat of the information contained in the original brochure and registration form. Small entry number slips were laid out on the tables, intended to prevent people from rearranging the entries so as to showcase their own.

It's certainly exhaustive Jessica thought to herself as she read:

Rules for entries

- Jars and lids should not show brand names.
- Jars should be cylindrical with vertical sides (not hexagonal, octagonal, bulbous, etc.)
- Jars must only be labelled with contents and detail the day, month and year made; labels should be half way up the jar and parallel to the base; they can be hand written or printed.
- Contents must reach within 3mm of top of jar.
- Polished external appearance with no finger marks.
- Seals must be airtight; twist tops preferred but waxed circles and cellophane are acceptable; not screw thread tops like on honey jars.
- 'Frilly hats' make **no difference** to the judge's decision which is based on flavour, texture and colour.

She turned around just as a tall man entered the room. He made an imposing figure, with a head of wavy dark brown hair, friendly green eyes and a full beard. He was wearing stout boots and a dark green tartan kilt, topped with a thick navy cable knit sweater. From the crook of his elbow swung a curved wicker basket lined with a bright red gingham, within which nestled three gleaming jars.

"Morning, Ealisaid! A fine job you're doing here."

Jessica recognized the man instantly as the MacNaughton of Castle Drummond. She had heard and read plenty about him since arriving in Dalkinchie. He was the Clan Chief of Clan MacNaughton as well as the Laird of Drummond, living in Castle Drummond in Dalkinchie's neighbouring village. She knew that he managed a medium-sized estate, owning land in both Drummond and Dalkinchie, some of which was given over to tenancy smallholdings – crofts, as they were known in Scotland. He appeared in the local paper for one reason or another almost every week, but this was the first time she'd seen him in person, and she watched with frank curiosity as he registered the preserves in his basket.

"Good morning, Mr MacNaughton. This'll be Margaret's jams and marmalade?" Ealisaid had already begun to scan her list.

"Aye, that it is right enough. Name of Mustard, Margaret Mustard, her entry number will be on the list but I have it here somewhere too if you need it…" He began to unclip his sporran, the leather purse Scottish men wore on a chain around their hips when wearing the kilt, but Ealisaid waved him away.

"No, no, I have it here. One pot blaeberry jelly, one pot raspberry and rhubarb jam, and one pot of the famous orange and whisky marmalade."

"All present and correct, Ealisaid! Usual place…right, right, I'll just pop them over here and I've to head off, I've got to see a man about some sheep, and then I'll be back at 11 for the woodwork judging."

The big bearded man delicately placed the jars on the judging table, smiled at Jessica and Ealisaid and then left, nodding cheerfully to another man who had just entered the room carrying a cake and with a sturdy-looking woven cloth bag awkwardly slung over his arm. "Donald."

The man nodded back. He matched the MacNaughton for height, but that was where the similarity ended. He was a portly man, wearing an ill-fitting pale grey suit, white shirt and tartan tie. Despite his relatively formal dress, the overall impression was of dishevelment – thinning grey flyaway hair, a florid face, shirt straining and escaping from the waistband of his trousers and splashes of mud on both his lower trouser legs and his shoes.

"Gillespie."

Minimal greetings achieved, the man turned to Ealisaid and said:

"One Victoria sponge and two pots of marmalade under the name of Donaldson. A lime, and an orange." He stood with barely concealed impatience, tapping his foot.

Jessica knew that the cakes registration had already closed, and wondered how her friend would handle this. Also, was the man's name really Donald Donaldson? Although come to think of it, his name sounded familiar, as if she had heard it recently. Where could that have been?

"Mr Donaldson, I'll register these for you, but the Victoria sponge should really have been here during the cake registration, from 8 – 8.30am. This is the preserves slot, 8.30 – 9am." She gestured to the large clock on the wall, and below it, the timetable for class registration. It was five minutes to nine in the morning.

"That's absolutely ridiculous. Are you saying you would expect me to queue up to submit the cake, then leave and come back twenty minutes later to register the jam?

Ealisaid's tone was conciliatory, born of years of experience of excellent customer service. "I know it's an inconvenience, and it might not seem logical, but technically yes, that would be how you would register goods in two different class groups. We try to minimise overlap for those who are entering goods in different parts of the hall, but sometimes it's impossible to avoid. Of course, you can register three item within a class all in one go. However, just this once we can overlook it and I'll register Mrs Donaldson's cake along with her preserves. It can be our secret – if you promise not to tell Mr Wilcott, neither will I."

Ealisaid's attempt at humor fell flat. If anything, it only served to annoy Mr Donaldson further. His already pink face darkened to an angry puce, and flecks of spittle issued from his lips as he next spoke.

"Young lady, Desmond Wilcott is a long and trusted associate of mine, and I can assure you he would not take issue with this at all. He would agree with me absolutely that the way you are running things here makes no sense – no sense. Expecting people to queue up twice! It's scandalous, that's what it is – scandalous. You must think people have nothing better to do!"

Ealisaid remained unperturbed. "I didn't make these rules, Mr Donaldson. As head judge and show convenor, Mr Wilcott did. I'll make sure to give your feedback at the post-show committee meeting, and perhaps next year we can consider merging the edibles class into one. It's something I have suggested in the past. In the meantime, why don't you add your wife's cake to the table there, and her jam on the preserves table under the window. Registration is closing shortly and we will be setting this room up for judging."

Scarcely mollified, and clearly determined to have the upper hand, Mr Donaldson hissed "It's marmalade!" However, he then did as Ealisaid had requested, first with the cake – which was a beautiful-looking sponge, Jessica noted, standing lightly golden and proud inside its domed stand – and then turning his back on the two young women to place the marmalades in their appropriate places on the preserves table, taking his time to find the correct entry numbers. Jessica, making eye contact with Ealisaid behind his back, raised her eyebrows and in return Ealisaid rolled her eyes slightly. They quickly dropped their gaze as Mr Donaldson turned back round. He left without acknowledgement, responding only to Ealisaid's pleasant "goodbye, now" with a muttered "harrumph!" Leaving the room, he turned right towards the main Village Hall door just as the MacNaughton had done. Ealisaid watched him go, and then moved over to the window to check that he had definitely left the building.

"Jessica, close the door."

Jessica glanced at the clock. It was two minutes to nine.

"I know it's early, but I think that's everyone on my list. I'll just check – " Ealisaid flipped the pages on her clipboard, " – yes, everyone has entered. There's no-one else to come. Close the door, and I'll answer any questions you have for your article but I'll have to be quite quick – I want to get down to the café and check that Murdo and Mairead have managed to open up OK."

Jessica did as she was asked, but when she turned to Ealisaid it was clear that her friend had other things she wanted to address first.

"Did you get a load of Donald Donaldson there? Honestly. What a massive sense of entitlement. It's normally his wife that drops off her own entries and she's more than happy to queue up twice. She gets a nice chat in the queue, and if that's what she has to deal with at home, she probably is quite pleased to have a break! As for people having better thing to do – please. It's an hour or so out of your day. He's probably just going to play golf for the rest of it."

Ealisaid looked at Jessica and broke into a giggle. "This is all off the record, OK?"

Jessica smiled. "Of course. Look – no notebook, no recorder."

"Good. Thing is Jessica, he's right. It is a bit daft you are not meant to bring the cakes and jams at the same time. You'll find that it's the same people likely to enter both, and I could easily manage it – you see the set up here, it's no' exactly complicated! Through in the big hall, where they have big items and multiple classes, it makes more sense in there. In here I think they should merge them. I'll say so – again – at the next meeting. Right. So – on the record now – what would you like to ask?"

Jessica flipped out her notebook and went through her list quickly, noting down Ealisaid's responses as she went. She wanted a clear idea of the process, and general impressions of the number of entries, variety, the percentage of regular entries. Once she had captured that, she asked Ealisaid about the table set-up and the judging.

"It used to be we had enough volunteers to place the entries as well, although it made it a bit complicated – this isn't a very big room and people would argue over the placement. A few years ago we adopted this method of putting the entry numbers out and I must say, it works well. Sometimes people move things about to centre theirs, so I usually have a wee glance over – the numbers should just be in order. You can do that check with me if you like then I'll need to be away – I did promise I would check in on the café before I come back for the judging."

The two women ran their eyes over the cake table, checking for consecutive numbers and, in Jessica's case at least, admiring the variety and display of local talent. Deliciously light golden sponges vied for attention with rich, tempting chocolate cakes. Fruit loaves thickly studded with cherries and nuts…Dundee cake…syrupy drenched lemon and orange cakes, and several plates of scones, looking somehow both substantial yet melt in the mouth.

"What happens to the cakes afterwards?" asked Jessica. She knew that for the next two days the traditional crafts would be sold, some for significantly high prices, drawing aficionados from near and far. The cakes would be past their best by then though.

"Entrants have a choice. They can take them home today at 2.30pm after the judging, or they can slice, bag and sell them later today with all proceeds donated to the Craft Society. If I wasn't on the committee I suppose I would worry about the competition, but luckily the appetite for cakes never seems to drop away."

Jessica nodded and they moved over to the preserves table. Her eye was drawn immediately to the large curved jar that stood out, flagrantly breaking the straight-sided jar rules and – she looked closer – bearing an ornate oval printed label that read:

Castle Drummond Finest Blaeberry Jelly

She glanced along the table. Two other entries in identical jars, with labels that read:

Castle Drummond Orange & Scotch Whisky Marmalade
Castle Drummond Finest Raspberry Jam

The labels also reproduced a rough pen and ink sketch of the castle below the names and above the dates. A coat of arms was stamped on the metal lids.

Ealisaid saw her looking and smiled.

"You'll have noticed yet more rule-breaking? Don't worry, this one is also permitted by our esteemed head judge. He's a real stickler for the rules, apart from when local men with influence want to bend them. Funny, that."

"So these were the ones submitted by...?"

"The MacNaughton, yes. You'll have noticed him? Every year. Margaret Mustard is his part-time housekeeper, see, and she makes her jams at the castle – says that it works far better in the ancient jeely pots on the big stove in the kitchen there, but also believes that this gives her the right to stamp 'Castle Drummond' all over them. You cannae blame her really, it's a brilliant marketing tactic."

Ealisaid paused in appreciation of Margaret Mustard's business acumen.

"Gillespie disnae mind, as long as he gets to eat it. He's got an awfy sweet tooth. Anyway, she always sends him in with the entries. Her excuse is that she also enters in the textile classes every year, and she cannae be in two places at once. She never swaps and sends him to register her knitting, though! She's a canny one, right enough. Mr Wilcott turns a blind eye. He wouldnae want to get on the wrong side o' the Laird of Drummond Castle. That would be pretty difficult; Gillespie's as kind a man as you'll ever meet. But there we are. I wouldnae mind, but – "

Despite the fact they were alone in the room, with the door closed, Ealisaid drew nearer to Jessica and said in a whisper:

"This is *definitely* off the record: Margaret Mustard wins every year, as well."

2

A Judging Calamity

After this dramatic piece of gossip Jessica and Ealisaid left the side room and the latter locked the door, so as to leave the entries undisturbed until judging time when she would return after working in her café for a couple of hours. Ealisaid had support in her café from her younger sister Mairead and her employee Murdo Smith, but the former was still only a teenager and the latter worked only very part-time at *Lissa's*, spending the rest of his time supporting his father on Balnaguise, the family dairy farm. He also volunteered as a Special Constable for the police force. Jessica wanted to take in the atmosphere of the big hall and see the registration of other craft classes, for her notes.

As the two women said their goodbyes, a middle-aged couple entered in the main door of the Village Hall. He had close cropped grey hair and flinty eyes, and walked slightly ahead, thin-lipped and unsmiling, dressed in a dark grey severely tailored suit. She was trailing behind with a tissue paper wrapped bundle held in her arms. Petite and fine-boned, with bobbed silvery hair, she had an elegant way of moving despite her armful, and a strained expression etched on her pale face. With them floated a cloud of tension, and Jessica thought that perhaps their entry into the building had cut short an argument.

The man nodded grimly at Ealisaid as he passed, heading straight for the main hall. The woman made no eye contact as she followed him to the same room. Neither said anything. Ealisaid waited until they were safely out of earshot before saying quietly to Jessica:

"And that was your head judge and show convenor, Mr Desmond Wilcott, along with his wife, Patricia. She's a very talented lacemaker and will be entering something in that class I should think. Her husband doesn't judge that one, so it's always allowed."

Jessica's eyes widened as she took in this new information. So that was the Desmond Wilcott she had heard so much about. He certainly fitted the description of someone methodical, orderly and unbending.

"Is he always that unfriendly?"

"He's never a warm man, but I'm surprised he didn't stop to talk, even if just to ask about how the registration went this morning. He would normally have been here earlier, too. If I hadn't detected an atmosphere I would have introduced you, Jessica. Maybe something has happened."

Maybe it has thought Jessica, looking again down the corridor to where the couple had disappeared into the main hall. Perhaps it was her imagination, but she still felt the chill of their passing in the air, and was nervous about what she might find if she followed them.

* * *

She needn't have worried. Upon entering the main hall herself, any hint of the tension they had picked up on between Desmond Wilcott and his wife had completely dissipated – in fact, the hall was so busy and full of people that she had trouble placing them at first. When she did spot them they were apart, Mrs Wilcott lining up to register her lacework, and the head judge clearly making up for lost time by doing a whistle-stop tour of the various stands, exchanging a few words with entrants and other committee members, then moving on quickly. Jessica flipped out her notebook. She was glad she would have the opportunity later to see the exhibits without any people in the way, as the present crowds were too thick for her to get a proper look at many of the crafts. Instead she tried to capture the impression of industry and optimism that hung over the show already, as well as an idea of the range of talent that was there in the different classes and categories. After two months in Dalkinchie, Jessica was still just getting used to the way that small communities could pull together to deliver a big event, and the importance of these events to the lives of the people of Dalkinchie, Drummond and further afield.

After a short time, Jessica took her notebook and her thoughts and disappeared into the newspaper office next door. *The Dalkinchie & Drummond Herald* occupied half of the upper floor of the building directly adjacent to the Village Hall. It was another weathered grey stone building with polished floor hallways. The local library took up the entire first floor. The newspaper shared the second floor with a small museum, staffed entirely by volunteers, and a small communal kitchen for tea breaks. Far from the sleek offices Jessica had vaguely pictured when she had first considered becoming a journalist, the newspaper offices were crammed into two rooms – one which was used by the editor Grant Mack, and the other, larger room for anyone else working for the newspaper on a freelance or salaried basis. Both rooms were haphazardly furnished; the computer equipment was a few years out of date but was perfectly serviceable, and Jessica had found herself enjoying working there enormously over the last couple of months. She had started with a profile on her aunt's new shop, and since then had contributed something every week.

The Craft Show was her biggest piece to date, and Jessica wanted to take every opportunity to type up her notes, knowing that she could polish them into something better in the coming days. Ignoring the post-it note stuck on the desk informing her that Nicholas Pringle had called – she could call him back later – she set an alarm on her phone so that she wouldn't forget to head back to the Village Hall for the judging, and set to work.

* * *

Forty-five minutes later Jessica nipped to the kitchen to get a glass of water and as she emerged, she became aware that there was someone talking in the hall below. The woman was speaking on her cell phone in a low voice and Jessica, feeling that she did not want to be overheard, stood helplessly still for a moment, knowing that if she moved she would betray her presence, but if she remained she would be eavesdropping. In doing so, she could not help but hear what transpired.

"Hello? Hello, it's Patricia Wilcott here. I'm calling about a flight reservation to Australia that I had made. Yes, I can hold."

A moment's silence. Jessica, acutely uncomfortable, backed quietly into the kitchen and pulled the door to, but she could still hear Patricia Wilcott below.

"Hello. Yes, yes, that's right. Yes, you're correct, the flights were cancelled yesterday, but I am calling now to check and see if it would be possible to re-book...no, just for myself this time. Mr Wilcott won't be flying with me. Yes, the same dates if at all possible please. Mmm-hmm. The same price, that's wonderful. Very good news. I'll come in and collect the tickets, please don't post them. Can I also use a different payment card please? No, not the one used previously. That's right. Oh, if you can hold them, that would be wonderful. I'll come in and pay later on today, or Monday at the very latest. Thank you so much. Goodbye."

With that, Patricia Wilcott ended her call and quietly stepped out of the building, allowing Jessica to ease the kitchen door open, and return to the newspaper office to work. She still felt mildly weird about having overheard the woman's vacation plans, but it didn't seem like anything too personal, fortunately. She had no doubt found the hall next door too noisy to make the call and had just nipped in next door for the peace, rather than for privacy. Jessica soon put it out of her mind and went back to work.

At just before 11am, Jessica met Magnus Smith outside the Village Hall. He carried a large camera bag over one shoulder.

"Hi Magnus, how are you?"

"Morning, Jessica! Fine, thanks for asking. How's things with you?"

Magnus, like his younger brother Murdo, worked primarily with the herd of Ayrshire dairy cattle on Balnaguise, their father's dairy farm. He was also *The Herald's* main photographer, fitting in freelance jobs around his daily schedule. Jessica had enjoyed the few occasions upon which work had thrown them together, finding Magnus relaxed and approachable...and easy on the eye. The lads had both inherited Dairy Smith's reddish wavy hair and frank blue eyes, and Jessica also appreciated how laid-back Magnus was, especially in comparison to her ex-boyfriend Mike who could not have been said to be chilled out about anything. Magnus was also an extremely talented photographer, and Jessica had wondered what he shot in his own time when he wasn't working for the paper. She would love to see more of his work.

"I'm good, thanks! I went round the show earlier when they were setting up and I've been writing for the last couple of hours. I'm looking forward to this. Have you worked at the Craft Show before?"

"Aye, it's a regular annual feature. Most of my work is, to be honest. There's a lot of tradition here, the same events year after year. This one is a big deal for Drummond and Dalkinchie, and a lot of folks around here."

They continued chatting as they moved into the main hall, transformed since earlier. The atmosphere was expectant and yet peaceful, the air thronged with possibility. Now that entrants had left the building, the room held all exhibits organised in their different classes and categories, helpfully labelled with the class description. The only other people present were the class judges, moving around the hall in small groups and conferring in low voices.

Jessica made a slow clockwise turn around the hall, making sure she had seen every class and would be able to put them in context later. The textile crafts included knitting, handloom weaving, and something called New Pitsligo Lace which, as Jessica discovered from the description, originated from a town in Aberdeenshire. An adjacent display board showed photographs of the process, both historical and contemporary. She marveled at the intricacies of the patterns and the delicacy of the craft, winding and knotting gossamer-thin thread through a detailed arrangement of pins, requiring the maker to keep track of multiple finely carved bobbins at once.

There was also a stand set up for show visitors to have a try at spinning yarn – either by hand using a drop spindle, or with a spinning wheel. Jessica stroked and squished the beautifully soft samples and admired the Eriskay ganseys – cozy fisherman cable knit sweaters, made to a pattern developed on the Hebridean island of Eriskay. She hadn't yet spent the winter in Scotland but could see how a gansey could be a very appealing addition to her wardrobe. The woodwork class included carving – both practical items such as lace bobbins, spoons and bowls, and decorative animals and birds – as well as small pieces of furniture. Jessica was particularly taken with an Orkney chair, handcrafted with a decorative straw seat, a high woven back and sides, and a small wooden drawer set in between the chair legs.

"I've heard they make them like that because of the awfy windy weather up in Orkney." Magnus had followed her over to the woodwork classes, and now took a photograph of the chair, positioning himself and his camera perfectly to catch the best light. "Coorie yourself in one of those, a blanket, a bottle of whisky in the drawer, and you'd be just fine."

Jessica laughed. "Not a bad idea. Have you ever been to Orkney?"

"I have not. I would love to one day, though. I've heard it's a wonderful place. Incredible photography opportunities too, and there's always that chance of catching the Merry Dancers."

"The Merry Dancers?" This was an unfamiliar term to Jessica, but she was intrigued.

"The aurora borealis. Northern lights. There's folk that go to Orkney, or even all the way up to Shetland, just in the hope of seeing them. There's no guarantees, but a better chance than hereabouts. They're meant to be tricky to photograph but I wouldnae mind the opportunity to try. One day."

He smiled at Jessica, and moved off to get a close-up shot of some basketwork in the willow weaving category. Jessica looked after him for a moment, briefly allowing herself to daydream. One day. She was pulled up short by her phone alarm buzzing inside her pocket. 11.25 am. Time to head back to the cakes and preserves, where the judging was about to start.

Entering the small room, Jessica saw that the three judges had already taken their place behind the table. Ealisaid, her long dark hair pulled back in a ponytail, sat in the middle, flanked by Desmond Wilcott on her right, and the third judge on her left – a woman Jessica recognised as a member of the local Women's Guild. Each judge had a glass of water in front of them.

The table was covered with a snowy white thick tablecloth, and the judges were attended by two stewards who displayed each cake in front of them before preparing and serving the cake samples, and taking the remainder away. The cakes were referred to only by their entry numbers as they were passed to the judges, and the judges' forms contained only the reference numbers as well.

The cake judging proceeded remarkably quickly, as the three judges nibbled, conferred, and made notes. Jessica couldn't make out what they were writing; although Desmond Wilcott wrote in a distinctive spiky script, it was too far away to be legible. She noted the calm atmosphere, the lack of dissent between the judges and the speed at which everybody moved through their tasks. Clearly this operation had been running well for a number of years and everybody knew exactly what their roles were.

Once the cakes class was finished, the three judges took a short break, standing up to stretch their legs before returning to judge the preserves. The stewards refreshed the water glasses and started to prepare the preserves for judging. The format was slightly different here, as the jams and marmalades had to be scrutinised while still in the jar to check for overall presentation and appearance as well as color and clarity. Ealisaid had explained that while translucency was a sought-after quality, too much could indicate that the sugar content was too high. Desmond Wilcott would take a jar and hold it by the lid up to the light, looking it over thoroughly and making notes before passing it to his fellow judges, who did the same. The jar would then be passed back to the head judge who would open it for tasting. Each judge would use a clean spoon to place a dollop of the jam or marmalade on to an individual saucer in front of them, checking for consistency as they did so. Jessica knew that it should have a 'good set', not syrupy, and that for marmalade, the peel should be very soft. Lastly, aroma and flavour were critical. Each judge would have their own preferences here, but they were looking for true flavours to match the fruit description, and if anything else had been added, it shouldn't overpower the fruit.

Once they were set up, the preserves judging went as smoothly as the cake judging had. Again, Jessica couldn't read their expressions as they stirred, tasted and made notes. None of them gave anything away. When Margaret Mustard's distinctive Castle Drummond Marmalade was brought to the table, Jessica perked up. Hadn't Ealisaid said that this one always took first place? Maybe she would be able to pick something up in their reactions to this tasting session.

Desmond Wilcott went through the same process as he had for all the preserves. Hold the jar up to the light, turn it slowly to view from all angles. Jessica could really see now why there such strict regulations on jars – there was no hiding whose entry this was. He passed it down the table to his fellow judges who repeated his actions and made notes. Jessica made a mental note of her own to ask Ealisaid later what she really thought about Margaret Mustard's marmalade. The jar was passed back and Desmond Wilcott opened it with a satisfying 'pop!' before spooning the golden preserve out on to his saucer. He pulled the back of his spoon across the marmalade and tested a piece of peel with its edge before passing the jar down to Ealisaid. He was raising the spoon to his lips as Ealisaid lifted the jar and took a delicate sniff at the contents, before she dipped her own spoon into the jar.

Jessica watched. Desmond Wilcott had tasted his sample spoonful now and made a short note, before swallowing some more, upon which he seemed to catch his breath. And again: a short cough, or gasp. He glanced up, and briefly made eye contact with Jessica. His eyes were wide, staring, and now he dropped his spoon from his right hand and grabbed at his arm. His face reddened, but he hadn't made much of a sound. The jar had been passed to the third judge. Ealisaid lifted her spoon to her lips.

"Ealisaid – don't taste that!" Jessica's shout to her friend was panicked, but she needn't have worried because as Desmond Wilcott continued to gasp, Ealisaid dropped the spoon and turned to him. The third judge, pushing both the jar and her saucer of marmalade away, stood up in alarm.

"Mr Wilcott's choking…is it a piece of peel? Mr Wilcott, have a glass of water. Mr Wilcott!" The young steward was trying to be helpful, but as she proffered the glass to Desmond Wilcott, his arm flailed upwards and knocked it out of her grasp. The glass arced over the table, landed a glancing blow on its edge and clattered to the floor but fortunately didn't smash; water drenched the tablecloth in front of him.

Ealisaid had thumped him firmly on his back. "Try and cough, Desmond," she was saying steadily, but he either wouldn't or couldn't. He then seized the tablecloth, which was slowly half-dragged from the table, the saucers and spoons with it, as Mr Wilcott slid off his chair and collapsed, both Ealisaid and the steward struggling to support his fall from either side.

"Call an ambulance!" Ealisaid's voice was authoritative, her command directed at the second steward, a young lad by the name of Callum. He nodded, wide-eyed, and left the room. Jessica went with him, stood in the hall and held the door closed behind her, looking around wildly and hoping that the caretaker might be there. Wouldn't they be trained in first-aid? Would they have any useful equipment? She knew Ealisaid, as a climber, had some training.

Callum had finished his call. "The ambulance is on the way. Will I go and see if I can find the caretaker, Miss?"

Jessica realised that he was deferring to her as the most capable adult around.

"Yes. See if they have a first-aid kit – whatever they have. If you can't find them, but you see Magnus Smith, ask him to come to the room. Don't let everyone know though, we don't want them all to start to panic."

"Yes, Miss."

Callum ran off towards the main hall. Jessica returned into the room where she found the other young steward almost in tears, the third judge comforting her, and Ealisaid trying to perform CPR.

"He's…. unconscious, Jessica."

Ealisaid could barely get the words out in between her efforts. Jessica ran over to assist and as she did so, Magnus arrived at the door of the room.

"What's going on?"

"It's Desmond Wilcott! He's had a stroke, or a heart attack…or something…" and Jessica's eyes met Ealisaid's across his prone body, and then slowly they both turned their gaze to the domed pot of Castle Drummond Orange and Whisky marmalade, sitting untroubled on the judging table.

3

News Travels Fast

J essica and Ealisaid left the room after the paramedics
arrived, which gave them the opportunity to share their
suspicions.

"Ealisaid, that marmalade…he was totally fine before he tried
it! " Jessica kept her voice to an urgent whisper, but she wanted
to ensure her friend had seen the same events play out as she
had.

"I know." Ealisaid's expression was grim, concern drawing
together her eyebrows and pressing her lips together.

"Should we tell someone? Do something?"

"I dinnae know, Jessica. Hang on a wee minute, I'm just
thinking."

Ealisaid paused, clearly trying to decide what to do next. The
hall itself was still quiet, with the judges in the large hall unaware
of the drama taking place here in the corridor, and in the cake
and preserves judging room. Jessica knew that this was serious.
The show was huge, thousands of pounds worth of artisan crafts
sitting there in the main hall, hundreds of visitors expected in
just a few hours to begin a day of presentations followed by two

days of sales. Some people had traveled long distances to enter. It would be unthinkable to cancel, but the alternative – keeping going as normal when show convenor Desmond Wilcott was grievously ill – seemed equally unthinkable. Especially if it turned out that something he had eaten in the course of his duties was responsible.

Ealisaid spoke up. "I told the paramedics exactly what happened. They asked lots of questions, about what he'd had to eat – that was tricky! Also whether he was on medication, history of heart trouble…I didn't know the answers. I had to say he was married but that I didn't know where his wife was. They said that they would need to take him away, and to try and find her." She came to a decision. "The café. If she's not there, surely someone will know where she is. I doubt I'll get through if I phone though, Murdo and Mairead will be run off their feet on Show day. I don't feel I can leave here either. I'm Vice-Chair, and there will be a panic soon, when people find out about Desmond. That wee steward Ellie is already very distressed. I'll have to be in charge. We'll need to decide what to do about the Show."

"Down to the café? I'll go." Magnus had been standing near the whole time, half-listening to their conversation. Now he volunteered his help.

"Magnus, that would be great. I know it will be tricky, but be discreet; try and get hold of Patricia Wilcott or find someone who knows her and can contact her. Also – and I really hope I'm wrong about this – I think we need Murdo here. Tell Mairead I'm sorry, and I'd only do this if really necessary. I'll find her someone else to help in the café as soon as I can."

Magnus listened gravely. "On it, Ealisaid. I'll run there noo. Jessica, can you lock my camera next door in the office? It will only slow me doon."

He passed the shoulder bag to Jessica and took off.

Magnus' brother Murdo's role with the police meant that he had assisted in investigations before. Jessica knew that if Ealisaid was asking for Murdo, it could only mean one thing. She, too, suspected that the preserves judging room might be a crime scene.

* * *

Magnus arrived at *Lissa's* within a few minutes. Ealisaid had been right, the café, always popular on a Saturday, was packed with people – many locals, but also a number of people from out-of-town looking for a cup of tea and a slice of cake to while away the waiting, in between entering their crafts and the opening of the Show. Mairead and Murdo were coping fine, Mairead behind the counter taking orders and serving drinks and Murdo currently serving food orders out to waiting tables. Every table was full, and there was a queue waiting to be served as well.

It wasn't surprising. While Ealisaid's café didn't have much competition in Dalkinchie, it was a genuinely charming little establishment. Since taking on the café after her mother's death nearly ten years before, Ealisaid had worked hard to give it her own stamp with a cozy ambience, and an affordable yet delectable menu. She displayed Dalkinchie and Drummond artists on her limited wall space and sold a small selection of local produce too, including cheeses made from the Smiths' own Balnaguise milk. Her range of cakes was well known locally and she kept everyone in the village well topped up with hot drinks, including her own mild Dalkinchie roast coffee.

Magnus glanced around. He couldn't see Patricia Wilcott

31

anywhere, but spotted a couple of women whom he knew had entered textile crafts. The café was filled with the noise of chatting. He sighed. How to obey Ealisaid's instruction to be discreet? He decided to start with Murdo, watching for his brother who had disappeared into the kitchen with a tray of mugs in need of washing. When he re-emerged, Magnus stepped in front of him before he could reach the main body of the café.

"Murdo, can I have a wee word?" He kept his voice low, but it seemed that Murdo hadn't picked up on this because he responded, loudly and cheerily:

"It's yourself, Magnus! I thought you would be too busy to pop in the day. Were you not tied up with the photography at the Village Hall?"

"Aye, I was. That's why I'm here. There's been a…problem at the Village Hall. Ealisaid thinks you're needed, and maybe give your boss a wee call too."

Magnus was referring to Detective Inspector James Gordon, with whom Murdo had worked on a previous case in Dalkinchie.

"Aye, right enough, Magnus. If Ealisaid says I'm needed then I must be! I'm no sure it's a good idea to leave Mairead here on her own though. It's awfy busy and it's no' likely to calm doon any time before the Show opening. Would I have to go to the hall right away?"

"Aye, Murdo, I think you really should, it's quite serious. Tell you what, I'll stay here and help oot until Ealisaid can arrange for someone else to come in and help. She said she would. First I need to find Patricia Wilcott, the heid judge's wife. Do you ken where she is?"

Murdo took a long look around the café before responding.

"She's no' here, Magnus."

"Aye, I can see that. Has she been in though? This morning, I mean," Magnus added hastily, knowing his brother well, and understanding that he was likely to list all the occasions upon which Patricia Wilcott had ever visited the café.

"I cannae mind. I'll ask Mairead." And before Magnus could intervene, Murdo had called across to Ealisaid's younger sister, still serving drinks from behind the counter:

"Mairead! Have you seen Mrs Wilcott in at all this morning, or passing by?"

So much for discreet. Mairead indicated that she had not seen her, but it was too late: heads whipped round, the babble of noise receded, then just as swiftly restarted but this time it was all directed at Murdo – and Magnus.

"Did he say Patricia Wilcott? Who's looking for her?"

"Patricia's not here. She'll be at the show at 2.30pm, though."

"Who are they looking for?" This was a woman whom Magnus knew to be a little hard of hearing. Her companion had to raise her voice to get across to her.

"Patricia Wilcott, Dorothy!"

"Patricia Wilcott? She's thon judge's wife, the one who does the lace. Aye, she'll be entering the Show. She always does." Satisfied that this cleared the matter up, Dorothy returned to her scone, taking a nibble followed by a sip of tea.

Magnus felt he had to intervene. Discreetly.

"I've just come from the Hall and Patricia Wilcott is needed up there. There's a…wee problem, but we dinnae know where she went when the judging started. Can anyone contact her or know where she was headed?"

"What kind of a problem, Magnus, son?"

He should have known he wouldn't get away easily. Any

chance he had had of keeping this under wraps was over. He faced a room of curious faces, all looking directly at him and wondering what he would say next.

"Err, well, I just really need tae find her." Magnus was floundering. He didn't think there was any way of getting out of this conversation without telling the truth – or at least part of it. "Her husband has maybe been taken ill at the Show – we just want to let her know, but naebody up there had her contact details."

Again, the cacophony of responses.

"Desmond Wilcott's no' ill. I saw him myself this morning. He'll be at the Show, doing the judging."

"Taken ill? Why, whatever's the matter? Nothing serious, I hope. The Show opens at 2.30."

"Who's ill? Patricia Wilcott? Oh, dearie me." Dorothy shook her head before placidly supping more tea.

Magnus moved to stand in the centre of the café, trying once again to get his information across.

"You're right, he wis fine this morning, that's true, but I just came from the Hall right now. He took ill ten minutes ago, while judging the marmalade. It's a sudden thing. There's an ambulance been called. We need to reach his wife – does naebody know her number?"

"I do. Patricia's a friend of mine. I'll contact her right now." A quieter voice rose from the back of the café, from a woman in a green patterned raincoat, sitting alone at a small table. Magnus nodded in relief at the woman who immediately pulled out her phone and began to send a message. He turned to talk to Murdo, to tell him he could leave for the Hall straight away, but was interrupted again.

"Did you say he took ill while judging the marmalade, young

34

man?" At first Magnus couldn't tell who had spoken. No-one had arisen from a table.

"Sorry?" Magnus looked round in confusion, trying to pinpoint the speaker. It became clear that he had been accosted by the table of women sitting near the front, all of them members of the local Women's Guild. Margaret Mustard sat among the group. A tall, robust woman with a cloud of strawberry blond hair, she had become quite pink in the face and was blinking rapidly. Her chocolate eclair sat untouched in front of her.

"You said that judge Wilcott took ill while judging the marmalade."

"Did I? I dinnae know exactly, although aye, come to think of it there was a pot of marmalade sitting on the judging table when I came in to see what was going on. I must just have assumed that was what they were doing."

"Which pot of marmalade was it?" Margaret Mustard's voice was oddly high-pitched and hoarse. The women next to her patted her on the arm and said "now, now Margaret, I'm sure it's nothing at all. Desmond Wilcott keeps well, but I'm sure I've heard it mentioned that he has high blood pressure or something like that. That's what it will be..." but her voice trailed off as she saw the unwavering expression on Margaret Mustard's face and it became clear that she wasn't getting through to her.

Magnus shrugged. "I dinnae ken. It wis definitely marmalade, though, not a jam or anything. It was in a kind of a curved jar."

Margaret Mustard made a strangled sound, and abruptly stood up, amongst a flurry of concerned responses from her friends.

"It'll not have anything to do wi' your marmalade, Margaret!

Dinnae worry!"

Their entreaties made no difference. Margaret Mustard was determined she was going up the Village Hall to sort this out for herself. It was quickly decided that if Margaret was going, the rest of the group were going too.

Magnus watched them all leave the café, following Murdo up the High Street towards the Village Hall. He sighed, rolled up his sleeves and tied one of Ealisaid's trademark green tartan aprons over his shirt and around his waist. That could not be said to have gone according to plan. Och well – it wasn't as if much could be done about it now – *the tatties were ower the side*, as his father would say. He picked up a tray and went to clear the table that Margaret Mustard and her friends had just vacated.

He just hoped that the Village Hall could take what was coming.

* * *

Fortunately for Murdo, he arrived at the Village Hall a little before Margaret Mustard and her companions. Encouraged by Ealisaid and Jessica, and displaying some of the fortitude he had shown when last working with the police, he soon had the situation under control. With Detective Inspector Gordon contacted and on his way, Murdo had agreed that the circumstances were such that it would be a good idea to close off the room where Desmond Wilcott had collapsed. The ambulance had left for the hospital, unable to wait for Patricia Wilcott who hadn't yet arrived at the Hall. Murdo next turned his attention to the Women's Guild group, managing to convince most of them that they would best help Margaret by going about their day elsewhere, invoking the status of the judging and the fact that the Show wouldn't open until 2.30pm. He hadn't quite managed to get rid of them all, however.

"Margaret is looking for answers, young man! She needs reassurance that Desmond Wilcott's illness is not connected to her marmalade. We have been informed that it was the last item he tasted before he took seriously ill." Miss Janet Simpson spoke on behalf of Margaret, who stood off to the side, continuously wringing her hands, unable to ask questions or indeed speak coherently at all. Murdo responded very gently.

"Aye, well, I cannae comment on that, but I totally understand. Mrs Mustard, you must be awfy worried. I think the best thing would be if you had a wee quiet seat somewhere while we sort it all oot and wait and see what has to be done. Detective Inspector Gordon is on the way, and he'll have the best idea. Are you able to wait? We'll find you somewhere. I promise we will tell you any information we have as soon as we are able."

The upshot of this was that Ealisaid arranged for Miss Simpson to stay with Margaret Mustard in a quiet corner of the main hall, despite the fact that it was filled with crafts and ongoing judging. It seemed the best solution as they awaited further instruction upon the arrival of DI Gordon. Ealisaid, having decided that the Show had to go ahead in some form or another, was having many urgent low-voiced conversations with committee members and stewards about exactly what form that would take. When Patricia Wilcott arrived alone at the Village Hall, it therefore fell upon Jessica to meet her.

The entrance hall to the Village Hall building led directly to the large main hall, with two smaller rooms off to either side of the entrance hallway – the closed off judging room on the left, and a similar-sized room on the right. Often used for committee meetings, today the second room was the administrative centre of the Craft Show. Forms were processed here, prize cards printed and signage stored. Ealisaid had suggested that this might make the best venue for Patricia Wilcott when she arrived, and had asked a steward to open it up for them. Jessica, following her advice, escorted the judge's wife in. The room had been cleared of people so that Jessica and Mrs Wilcott could sit there, but it was cluttered, evidence of the running of the Craft Show all around them. Two tables, currently being used as desks in the centre of the room, held piles of paperwork. A third table, pushed back against the wall, contained a row of highly polished silver cups and trophies, in addition to a large cardboard box piled with multiple small two-handled carved silvery bowls. *Quaichs,* Jessica remembered, having seen the traditional Scottish drinking cup being used at Reenie's New Year's Eve party in Edinburgh one year. They must be handed out as prizes in the Show.

Jessica brushed aside a pile of papers and placed a glass of water for Patricia Wilcott on one of the tables. She pulled out two chairs and sat beside the woman. She had noticed her fine bone structure and air of insubstantiality earlier on that morning, but even since then Patricia Wilcott seemed to have shrunk and become more fragile, her thick cardigan emphasising the narrowness of her shoulders, her wispy hair falling lightly over her deep eye sockets and sharp cheekbones. She continued to be quite calm, taking the seat that she was offered and folding her hands in her lap. She kept up a stream of chatter, which surprised Jessica, although the latter felt that she was really just present for Patricia Wilcott's own internal monologue – she wasn't expected to say anything in return.

"I had just nipped to do some errands in the village. Thank

you for tracking me down. I don't have any car keys – Desmond had them – but I've managed to get hold of our solicitor, Donald Donaldson. He's also a close family friend. He can take me to the hospital and stay with me while I speak to the police. I was lucky he heard his phone, he was in the middle of a round of golf. I'll wait here until he arrives, or until the police do, whatever happens first.

"My friend told me that there's already a rumour flying around that Desmond was poisoned by something at the cake judging. At first I dismissed it, because that's ridiculous surely. But then I wondered – why all this fuss? The police have been called, and you've quite clearly closed off the judging room. He was certainly in perfect health this morning. He has no medical complaints, nothing unusual for a man of his age, anyway."

Patricia Wilcott continued to muse.

"Desmond isn't an easy man. He is very pedantic and particular, and he rubs people up the wrong way quite often. When he retired from the bank, there were quite a few people upset with him then because there had just been a big round of cuts and redundancies after the bank had been in trouble for some time. Desmond got to keep his pension, though. That put a few people's noses out of joint."

Jessica took the woman's hand gently. Did she really believe that someone could have harmed her husband on purpose?

Patricia spoke quietly. "He also has a long standing feud with a person in *The Herald* letters pages, just nit-picking backwards and forwards about various local issues. He's on a lot of committees and there are always falling outs and people resigning. That's just par for the course with these things, though. None of it is serious. I can't imagine that anyone would poison him for any of that! I can't imagine anyone would poison him at all, to be honest. It seems like such a – strange thing to do."

Jessica, unclear how to answer, simply patted Mrs Wilcott gently on her arm and continued to listen. Patricia Wilcott suddenly turned to her and said:

"You were in the room. Do you think he was poisoned? How would it even have been possible? I know Desmond's systems and I can't imagine how it could occur!"

Jessica struggled to respond. What to say to this woman, who seemed to be approaching the whole notion of her husband's potential attempted murder as a puzzle? She wondered whether Patricia Wilcott could be in shock, but was unsure what the symptoms of that could look like. Certainly there was an air of denial and other-worldliness about her response to the events. Jessica was sure it didn't mean much other than the fact that Patricia Wilcott had not yet fully processed what had happened.

At that point Detective Inspector Gordon arrived, and Jessica was grateful because it meant that she didn't have to answer Patricia's last question. DI Gordon didn't remark upon Jessica's presence in the room. Never a particularly cheery man, he looked especially solemn and, Jessica noticed, more tired than he had when she had met him a few months before.

Patricia Wilcott had stood up as soon as DI Gordon entered the room. Jessica followed her lead and stood up too, taking a respectful pace to the side as the Detective Inspector greeted Mrs Wilcott.

"I can tell by your face that it's not good news, Detective Inspector. Please, just tell me." And then, as DI Gordon shot a look at Jessica: "You can speak in front of Jessica. She's been very kind to me, staying with me and listening to my rambles while we waited to find out what was going on. I've greatly appreciated her company."

She looked at Jessica and briefly smiled, and Jessica felt a warm rush of empathy for her. How difficult it must have been to receive an urgent message and make her way up to the Village Hall, not knowing what she would find there, perhaps especially after she and her husband had argued that morning. And now it seemed that tragedy had struck, and the argument must stay unresolved for ever.

DI Gordon nodded and cleared his throat. His eyes shifted. Jessica, feeling uncomfortable, glanced towards the table and fixed her gaze on one of the lists there, trying to avoid making eye contact with either DI Gordon or Patricia Wilcott for this deeply personal news. The sheet was headed 'Class 14 Category 2: Vanilla Sponge – entries' and contained a printed list of digits that Jessica recognised as entry numbers. There were some short, handwritten notes around six of the strings of numbers. Jessica couldn't quite make out the notes, although they were written in Desmond Wilcott's distinctive, spiky handwriting, and many of them were followed by an exclamation point.

The clock ticked. DI Gordon spoke.

"Mrs Wilcott, I'm afraid I do indeed have to share bad news. I'm very sorry to have to inform you that your husband died in the ambulance on the way to the hospital."

Patricia Wilcott's hand flew to her throat where it trembled. She closed her eyes, but didn't speak, although her lips were moving soundlessly.

"Jessica, could you pass Mrs Wilcott that glass of water?"

Jessica, eager to help, picked up the glass, but Patricia Wilcott opened her eyes and said:

"No, no. I don't need water. I'll be fine in a moment," and then, leaning forward slightly, she fixed her eyes on the Detective

Inspector and said:

"What was the cause of death?"

"That's yet to be determined, Mrs Wilcott. We don't yet have all the information we need. In the meantime, do you have any family or friends that could come and be with you right now? You will be required to go to the hospital, but I don't recommend that you should go alone."

Mrs Wilcott's reply was quiet. "Our daughter – our only child – lives in Australia. I have a friend arriving soon though, and I'm sure he will take me wherever I need to be."

Australia thought Jessica, something falling into place, but at the same moment she heard the raised voice of Donald Donaldson outside in the entrance hall. "I'm looking for Mrs Patricia Wilcott!"

DI Gordon moved to escort Mrs Wilcott from the room, and just as she was about to leave she paused, turned to Jessica and said:

"Thank you, Jessica. I'm very grateful for your company and your kindness. You remind me a little of my daughter, you know."

Jessica nodded. "I'm very sorry for your loss, Mrs Wilcott."

Patricia Wilcott inclined her head, and then gracefully moved out into the entrance hall where she was greeted by Donald Donaldson. Jessica heard them discuss their next steps and then exit the Village Hall. She quickly scuttled around the table to have a better look at the list she'd seen. She had been right. This was an entry sheet, marked up with identifying names against the so-called anonymous entry numbers. What could it be used for, if not to sway the judging? Had Desmond Wilcott been using it to memorise particular entry numbers – to either ensure a win, or engineer a disqualification?

Voices outside the room drew her away from the table and out into the entrance hall, where DI Gordon was now speaking with Murdo and Ealisaid.

"I understand your concerns, Miss Robertson, but this could be the scene of a crime. At the very least, it's a sudden death. We are bound to investigate, and that won't be compatible with hundreds of people walking in and out."

"Hundreds of people have already been in and out, DI Gordon. We've been taking entries in since 6.30am, people walking in and out of the main hall and this room as well. I do have a list of everyone who came in to this wee room though – at least, I have a list of the entries, and I can remember who dropped them all off. We cannae close the Show. People have travelled miles, but apart from that, we've a hall already full of artisan crafts. We have limited event insurance, and we recommend that entrants get their own, but we dinnae insist upon it. The main issue is that even if we canceled, it's too late to get the word oot. There will be people here at 2.30 whether we like it or not, so we might as well be prepared for it. Edibles are canceled and we'll put signage up to say so. The cake and preserves room can stay locked off. The Show's meant to be open from 2.30 to 5.30pm with the announcements at 6pm, there's probably something I can do to make that shorter and limit the numbers. But I cannae stop people arriving."

DI Gordon looked serious, but didn't interrupt. Murdo glanced at Ealisaid and then took up the tale himself:

"The Craft Show's an awfy big deal in Dalkinchie and Drummond, sir! It's been running for generations...and there's generations of families who have always entered every year in the same categories as well. It brings a lot of people into the village. It can be controversial though. I mind that there was this one year, and Mrs Young entered the knitting and won a prize, and someone else – I think it wis Elsie McNab – said that she had stolen her pattern, and then someone else said that it didnae matter, because anything that Elsie knitted ended up looking like a dish-cloot anyway so it would never have won a prize, and Elsie took her knitting bag and she wis aboot tae wallop..."

"Yes, thank you, Constable Smith." DI Gordon, used to dealing with Murdo, concealed his exasperation well, thought Jessica. Secretly, however, she wanted to hear the outcome of the story about Elsie McNab and her knitting bag. She spoke up.

"Detective Inspector...if it's a case of needing a room to speak to people, the newspaper offices are next door and they are empty. I have a key. Also, I was here this morning, and I took lots of notes. Murdo's brother Magnus was here too from 11am, and he was taking photos in the Main Hall. I am not sure whether any of that helps, but I thought perhaps..." she trailed off.

"Thank you, Miss Greer. That does help. I will definitely need to speak to you both later on today, and will take you up on the offer of the newspaper offices, that sounds ideal. Miss Robertson, I think the best thing to do is go ahead with your plan. Open as normal, try and cut the show short and keep this room closed off. I imagine many people will already have heard about Mr Wilcott's collapse, although I'm also sure that won't put them off coming to the Show."

He paused, taking his phone from his inside breast pocket and glancing at it. "First of all I am going to have to organise a sample of that marmalade for extensive testing."

Unfortunately, as he spoke, Margaret Mustard and Miss Janet

Simpson had emerged from the Main Hall and made their way down the corridor. Clearly fed up with waiting, they had come out to find out what was going on for themselves, just in time to overhear DI Gordon's pronouncement.

"Testing...are you talking about MY marmalade? Is that what he said? Oh, heavens above! Oh Janet!"

The woman was alarmingly red in the face. Ealisaid, perhaps fearful of another casualty, rushed to her side and took her arm.

"Come away back in and sit down Margaret, I'm sure it's nothing, they just have to be thorough."

Jessica, glancing at DI Gordon's impassive face, was not convinced. If the Castle Drummond marmalade *was* poisoned, who could have done it?

4

A Walk in the Park

Once Margaret had recovered a little, Ealisaid had thought it prudent to walk her down the hill to the café, where she hoped to calm Margaret with some tea. It also meant that she would be able to relieve Magnus, sort out her staffing problem and return to the Village Hall as soon as she could, in order to further prepare for whatever version of the Craft Show would go ahead. Jessica accompanied them, carrying Margaret's handbag for her as the woman had complained of feeling 'wabbit'. Ealisaid had explained that this meant faint and shaky, and the two were not taking any chances. Margaret was a far more healthy color now, however, and in fact had kept up a steady pace as well as dominating the conversation all the way down the hill, almost without pausing for breath. Jessica and Ealisaid listened patiently. They didn't have much choice, for Miss Janet Simpson had taken her leave on their way down the High Street.

"Of course, I always make my marmalade at Drummond Castle. The Laird is more than happy for me to use his kitchen, and his muckle jeely pots. I'm not sure who would use them if

I didn't!"

Jessica wasn't sure what Margaret was driving at. She remembered that Ealisaid had already mentioned Margaret making her preserves in the MacNaughton's large pots, but what could it have to do with today's events? Was Margaret Mustard just bragging? But it became clear with her next sentence.

"And he's an awfy man, that Laird. Gillespie never locks his doors and he lets all and sundry away in, whether they've an appointment or no. I'll always mind the day I came into the kitchen and there was a pig under the table. A pig! He was meeting with a crofter, and for whatever reason, who knows what, the man had brought a pig with him. They all just came into the kitchen and then the Laird and the farmer went away upstairs to the study, and they just left the pig snuffling about in my...in the kitchens!"

Jessica made an appropriate surprised noise. Behind that, her brain was whirring. Was Margaret Mustard suggesting that someone else could have tampered with her marmalade in the Castle Drummond kitchens? Wasn't that jumping the gun a little – it hadn't even definitely been established that the marmalade had been the cause of death. It seemed a little early to be looking for a potential poisoner. It didn't seem as if Margaret Mustard agreed though. She had adapted with amazing speed, and was now positioning herself at the centre of an elaborate drama.

"Come to think of it, maybe I did notice someone skulking outside in the bushes when I was making the marmalade. I'm almost positive that I heard something; I was stirring and think I mind going outside to check. I thought whoever it was skedaddled quickly when I went out, but maybe they crept in to the kitchen and put something in my marmalade! Oh, heavens! Is someone trying to frame me? What would make anyone do such a thing?"

Jessica, pondering, asked:

"Did you only make the one pot of marmalade from that batch?"

"What? Oh no, of course not! I made about eight jars. It's Gillespie's favourite. I'm not sure what you mean. Oh I see, you are saying they couldn't have added something to the pot or the other jars would have been poisoned too. Maybe it was later on in the evening then, when the jars were setting and he just tampered with one of them. Come to think of it, I think it was later. That's right, the sun WAS low. What a wicked, wicked thing to do."

Ealisaid, eyes resolutely forward as she kept up the pace down the hill, replied.

"Right enough, Margaret. That will be something you should tell Detective Inspector Gordon later, when he wants to speak to you again. Just now I think you should try and put the whole thing out of your mind and have a cup of tea, and maybe a wee cake to go with it."

"That's a good idea, Ealisaid. You know, I hustled out of here so quickly earlier, I didnae even touch my eclair! Maybe it was partly low blood sugar that made me feel faint, I'm not used to missing my elevenses. I have a very early breakfast you know."

"No problem, Margaret, if Mairead didnae keep it for you we will get you another one, on the house. Come away in."

They had reached the door of *Lissa's* and Ealisaid pushed the door inwards, then held it for the older woman to go in first. Margaret Mustard was instantly greeted and fussed over by another table of older women, of which there seemed to be an inexhaustible supply in Dalkinchie. Jessica supposed that they were probably Women's Guild members as well. Just as Jessica was about to follow Margaret in to the café, Ealisaid leaned in and whispered:

"I don't know what you made of all that – oor Margaret has never shied from a drama. But I cannae help but think that she's worried folk will remember that she had a huge grudge against Desmond Wilcott."

* * *

Jessica didn't have much time to process this statement. Reenie, whose flower shop The Bloom Room lay directly across from *Lissa's* at number 12 Dalkinchie High Street, saw them arriving and nipped over, coaxing Willow on her red leash across the street after first, unsuccessfully, trying to get her to stop and sit at the side. Jessica, who was only just standing inside the door, went back out to meet her. Ealisaid had already whirled into action, serving customers, speaking to Magnus – who looked fine in his green apron – and Mairead, and reassuring everyone that yes, the Show would be going ahead.

"What on earth's been happening Jessica? I've had a few customers in the shop this morning that have mentioned a problem at the Craft Show. Has someone taken ill?" Reenie stood on the sidewalk outside the café. Willow nosed around their feet.

Jessica made a decision. "Let's walk Reenie, and I'll fill you in on what I know. Have you closed up the shop?"

"Yes, it's my lunch break. I was going to take Willow for a short walk to the park anyway. It would be lovely if you had time to join us." Still a young puppy, Willow was having regular walks of around twenty minutes so as not to put unnecessary strain on her developing muscles and bones. Jessica smiled at the excited pup, who was trying to jump up despite their attempts at training her. She crouched down and fondled the dog's silky ears.

"I have a little bit of time. Let's go."

Jessica and her aunt headed into the park, a large sweep of recreational land that ran through the centre of Dalkinchie. It contained a children's play park as well as numerous inter-connecting paths, rougher ground over adjacent fields, and smaller areas that had been individually landscaped by local community groups. The most direct path from Reenie's cottage to the village ran right through the park, and Jessica loved it. She was looking forward to exploring more of the intertwining pathways as Willow grew bigger and could cope with a longer walk. For now though, she was enjoying their frequent strolls and Willow's evident delight at all the new sensory experiences she was having.

The park was relatively busy today – at least, busy for small-town Scotland, which simply meant that it wasn't completely empty. As it was a Saturday and towards the end of the school holidays, there were plenty of children using the swings and slide in the play park as well as small groups hanging about by the Burn, a small river that wound its way through the green slopes. What an idyllic childhood, thought Jessica, having the run of the park for the whole summer. Parents pushed babies and toddlers in strollers, and there were quite a few other dog walkers as well, including some whose dogs could be trusted to run around off leash. Jessica couldn't imagine Willow ever being so mature, although everyone had told them that she would grow quickly. The trees were in full, lush leaf and the banks covered with yellow wildflowers and small pink thistles. Bees buzzed lazily around them.

As they walked, Jessica told her aunt about everything that had happened that morning. Reenie, always a good listener, didn't interrupt until Jessica had completely finished. It had been an uncharacteristically dry summer, and the route they took was cracked and uneven underfoot until it wound under the trees where the thick canopy of leaves had preserved the dampness of the bark path. Willow, not yet used to walking on a leash, darted this way and that, exploring smells, textures and every movement, meaning that both women had to be vigilant that she didn't wind in between their feet and trip them up. Reenie carried a pocketful of small treats to reward her every time she walked nicely for more than a few seconds in a row. Willow did not receive very many treats on this particular walk.

"Well, that's quite a lot going on. How terribly sad for Mrs Wilcott, and awful for the Show organisers too. It's not easy to arrange an event of that size and now I imagine they'll have to cancel, or what have they decided to do? I must call Grant. I know he was planning on bringing his mother down to the Show this afternoon. Would it be better if he didn't come?"

Jessica considered this. Grant's mother was an elderly woman who sometimes required a high level of care, especially if the situation was unpredictable. She also did get a lot out of her visits to village events though, and it would be a shame if people pulled out when Ealisaid was working so hard to ensure that there still was a Show to attend.

"Definitely call him, but the Show is going ahead so it's probably fine to bring Mrs Mack down for a short while. Ealisaid is crazy busy, but she has managed to arrange for a lower-key version of the Show. She'll be headed up there herself again shortly, once she has sorted out cover in the café. Murdo's been pulled away on police business. They will need to speak to us both because we were witnesses. I've arranged for that to happen in the newspaper offices. Actually, can you let Grant know I have done that, and I'll catch up with him a little later to work out what to do next?" Jessica had just realised that their feature on the Craft Show could probably not run as planned, and that she would need to have a conversation with Grant about the angle to take now that Desmond Wilcott – both Show Convenor and head judge – had died in suspicious circumstances during the judging.

Just at that moment, Jessica was accosted by a man who was garishly dressed, wearing burgundy pants topped with a knitted, diamond patterned vest over a green button-down shirt. His sandy-coloured hair was thinning on top, but he clearly spent a lot of time on his neat little moustache, apart from which he was clean shaven. Nicholas Pringle. She had completely forgotten to return his call; the events at the judging had put it out of her mind. He no doubt would not be very happy with her.

"Miss Greer! I'm glad to run into you." Nicholas Pringle looked with distaste at Willow, who was trying to jump up on him and whose paws and snout were less than clean after an active few minutes of scratching and rootling in the undergrowth beside the path. Reenie successfully managed to distract Willow with a treat. "Did you not receive my message?"

"Mr Pringle, yes I did. I'm sorry I haven't had a moment to get back to you. With the Craft Show, things have been busy…" Jessica trailed off, realising that unless she repeated the full story that she had just told to Reenie, the excuse sounded lame at best.

"Miss Greer, I do think that it's imperative that we meet to discuss the item you are writing for *The Drummond and Dalkinchie Herald.* I would hate readers to get the wrong impression of the meeting. If we could just go over some salient points and I could give you some assistance on the type of report that usually works best for these sorts of events. I understand that you are new to both journalism and the country, and might not have a firm grasps on how it works."

Reenie made a scoffing noise, and Jessica feared that her aunt might say something. Instead she spoke up herself. Truth be told, Nicholas Pringle had touched a nerve. She didn't have any formal training in journalism and, while she had enjoyed her work and the writing process over the last couple of months, she would be lying to herself if she didn't admit that she sometimes felt unqualified for the job, especially since aspects of the local culture were completely new to her. There's only so far a Scottish mother will get you.

She hadn't particularly felt nervous about this reporting job, though. It had seemed routine – a formal community meeting with minutes being taken. Grant hadn't allocated much space to it at all, meaning that Jessica had only focused on reporting the minimum details. She had considered it complete. Was she mistaken?

"Thank you Mr Pringle. I understand. Can you follow up with me in a couple of days? I'm completely tied up with Craft Show reporting at the moment."

"Not so tied up that you can't go for a walk in the middle of the day!"

This time Reenie did interject. "Everyone is entitled to a lunch break, Mr Pringle. Now if you'll excuse us, we will need to be getting back to the village."

Reenie's determined march would have been far more effective had Willow not protested at the sudden change of pace and dug her heels in. Nicholas Pringle was scarcely mollified, looking after them with exasperation. Jessica wondered if they had gone too far, but perhaps it was better to take a stand in the face of his rudeness.

On the return walk Willow did a little better, finally seeming to make the connection between the rewards in Reenie's pocket and her own behaviour. She trotted obediently at her owner's ankles for around twenty seconds before a pigeon alighted on the grass nearby causing her to bark and lunge, sending Reenie stumbling across the path despite the puppy's small size. Jessica smiled. Willow was a work in progress, just like Jessica's own career as a junior reporter.

Reenie and Jessica arrived back in the High Street, and Reenie returned to The Bloom Room with a promise to update Grant on the situation. Jessica moved back across the street to *Lissa's* where she could see from the outside that Ealisaid was still working. She could also see that Murdo and DI Gordon had arrived, presumably to arrange to speak to Ealisaid, Margaret Mustard and herself. As she entered the café she could tell that it was not going well. DI Gordon was standing at the front, trying to speak to the group of women sitting at the table with Margaret Mustard – who, Jessica noticed from the crumbs lying on the plate in front of her, had managed to finish her eclair this time around.

"I'll have you know that Margaret has been entering that marmalade for years – years, young man! Not once has there ever been any complaint whatsoever about the quality of her marmalade. In fact, it has been a top prize-winner on more than one occasion!" said Janet Simpson indignantly, clearly

Margaret Mustard's self-appointed champion.

"We just need to ask a few – "

"Margaret Mustard has been an absolute pillar of the community in Drummond and Dalkinchie – a pillar I say – since before you were in nappies. It's outrageous that she is being accused of this!"

"Mrs Mustard has not actually being accused of anyth – "

"You'll not find a more helpful woman than Margaret in these parts! She's involved in everything and works herself to the bone to make a better community around here. What have we come to, when you waste your time targeting innocent folk like Margaret while criminals just roam the streets in those cities, doing whatever they please! You'd be far better aiming your energies at them, and leaving decent, upstanding Dalkinchie folk alone."

"Can I just reiterate that – "

The situation seemed useless. The Women's Guild were too formidable in their high dudgeon. Jessica has never seen DI Gordon so flustered, or lost for words before.

Murdo intervened.

"Ladies, we don't want tae upset Mrs Mustard, but I think what DI Gordon is trying to say is that she might have valuable information which could help us find oot what happened."

This got a far better response than DI Gordon had, perhaps because most of the women present had known Murdo since he was a child and were inclined to look kindly upon him, or perhaps because Murdo's manner was less imperious and more conciliatory. Throughout the whole tirade Margaret Mustard had been quite content to sit there, taking as her due the praise that her friends heaped upon her. Now, however, she lifted both hands and made a calming gesture, while also saying in a noticeably martyred tone:

"I appreciate all your support ladies, I really do. However it is my *duty* to pass on any information to the police that might be useful in finding out who killed poor, unfortunate Desmond Wilcott. I have no doubt that it will be unpleasant, but I'm sure I have never been the type of person who shies away from her duty!"

Her friends demurred, "No indeed, Margaret. You certainly have not."

Margaret Mustard drew herself up to her full, stately height and said graciously: "I will come with you, Detective Inspector Gordon and Constable Murdo Smith. I will put my own feelings aside and do my duty to the community. I will assist in any way I can in the terrible murder of Desmond Wilcott."

"We don't know that it is a murder yet," said DI Gordon, but Murdo cut across him saying:

"We appreciate that, Mrs Mustard. We're awfy grateful. We'll do our best no' to keep you too long. Can you come away up the hill wi' us noo, to the newspaper offices? That's where we will hold the interviews."

Margaret Mustard inclined her head. "I can."

DI Gordon replied.

"Thank you, Mrs Mustard. Now, Miss Greer, Mr Smith – and Miss Robertson, if you would be so kind to join us as well. We will try to keep the interviews as brief as possible."

"Aye, that would be handy." This was Ealisaid, who had joined them from behind the counter. She had removed her green tartan apron and was able to leave the café because, finally, more support had arrived in the form of another young woman who Jessica recognized as one of Mairead's friends. Magnus looked relieved to be escaping his café duties, and removed his apron with alacrity.

Ealisaid continued: "Could you interview me first? It's approaching 2pm already, and in not much more than half an hour the Show will open and we will have hundreds descending on the Village Hall. I'll need to be there to keep an eye on things and tell them…something about what happened this morning."

"There's no need to tell anyone anything unless they ask, Miss Robertson. However, if they do then you can tell them that Mr Wilcott has died and that the police are simply looking into the circumstances surrounding his death. That shouldn't cause too much alarm."

Jessica couldn't help but feel that the Detective Inspector was badly mistaken.

5

The Wrong Marmalade

Jessica fell into step beside Murdo on the route back up to the newspaper offices. Ahead, Magnus talked to Ealisaid, and DI Gordon had positioned himself at the front to set the pace. However, he was matched by Margaret Mustard beside him who had been striding up and down Dalkinchie High Street for decades. Jessica felt that she could see DI Gordon struggling a little to keep up with her speed – and her conversation. She smiled to herself.

"How are you doing Murdo? Are you happy to be involved in another police case?" Jessica asked. Murdo had long harbored an ambition to do the work, but didn't want to join the police formally because he was needed on his father's farm, and enjoyed that work too. As they walked up the hill, their conversation was punctuated by Murdo greeting everyone they passed by name, and in many cases, exchanging a line or two as well. He was a well-liked character in Dalkinchie.

"Oh, aye. It's good tae feel like you are making a difference. It's always a terrible tragedy when something like this happens, but it'd be even worse, I think, if you didnae get answers and know that justice was done."

Jessica pondered this. Murdo was probably right, and once again she admired his ability to cut straight to the heart of the matter. Murdo could seem what her aunt would call 'away with the fairies' at times, but she was realizing that he could be amazingly perceptive when the situation demanded. He continued:

"Mrs Wilcott earlier, she wis ever so grateful when we spoke to her at the hospital. She's away back to the Donaldsons noo, they'll look after her for a bit. Her only child disnae live around here any more."

Jessica nodded. She remembered, the daughter was in Australia. She also remembered Donald Donaldson, blustering into the registration room that morning, demanding that the rules be bent for him. Try as she might she found it hard to think of him as a friend of the refined, softly spoken Mrs Wilcott.

"Have the families always been friends?"

"Aye. Donald Donaldson's a family solicitor, and the Donaldsons go back in Dalkinchie for generations. They've always had a law business here. The Wilcotts moved up here for Mr Wilcott's job at the bank, must be twenty years ago noo. They always moved in the same circles – the Golf Club mainly – and they each have one daughter of about the same age, Helen Wilcott and Nancy Donaldson. The girls went through the school together, a year younger than me. Holidays away as well. Since he retired, Mr Wilcott has been spending more time golfing, and Donald wis his golf partner more often than not. He's no' retired, but it didnae seem to matter. They've both competed in wee local tournaments and the like; Mr Wilcott wis a bit better than Donald Donaldson."

Jessica realized that this must be why the name Donald

Donaldson had rung a bell. As a diligent new member of staff, she had been reading every word that *The Herald* printed, including all the sporting results that she didn't understand.

Could the Golf Club have anything to do with the mysterious death?

* * *

Jessica ran ahead a little as they reached the newspaper offices, knowing that she would have to unlock the office doors. The layout of the offices made it ideal for interviewing multiple people, she realised. Grant's office was the inner of the two rooms, accessed only through a door from the outer office. It contained a very large wooden desk, which Grant kept clear and tidy, although the rest of the office was cluttered with decades of work. The outer office where Jessica normally worked contained a battered leather sofa as well as two desks, multiple shelving and filing units, a couple of printers and an old microfiche reader on a dedicated workstation in one corner. Grant had told Jessica he would show her how to use it to access old copies of *The Herald* for research. Jessica and Margaret waited here while Ealisaid moved into the inner office with Murdo and DI Gordon. A text from Grant had confirmed that he was happy with this arrangement, and would catch up with Jessica later. Magnus had gone to check on signage in the Village Hall next door, promising to return as soon as he was able.

Margaret Mustard struck up a conversation as soon as the heavy wooden door of the inner office closed behind Ealisaid.

"Well, it never rains but it pours, doesn't it?"

Jessica knew that this expression meant that bad things happen all at once, but couldn't really understand how it applied to this situation. Luckily, she wasn't expected to contribute:

"First, Janet's cat goes missing. He's a terror for wandering, and he usually turns up after a day or so, but it has been a week now and not a sign! She's put up posters, put the word out on that Facebook and she's taken to just rapping on people's doors and asking them to check their garage and sheds right there and then. Shameless! She won't take no for an answer. She's awfy fond of that cat, too fond if you ask me. I've told her manys a time. 'Janet,' I've said, 'you spend more on that cat's dinner than you do on your own!' But she'll no' be told. Well anyway, as I say, first it was that, then poor old Dorothy McMaster's arthritis had an awfy bad flare up again, she's a wee bit better now, but she was housebound for a couple of days there, poor soul. I was in and out all the time, wi' her soup, her laundry. And now this. Mr Wilcott collapsing and dying right in the middle of judging the Show. It'll be the talk of the toon. And my marmalade at the centre of it all!"

Jessica marvelled at the woman's ability to put *herself* at the centre of it all. After all, it seemed that the only factor connecting these events was Margaret Mustard. She tried to make appropriate *mmm-hmm* noises, hoping that Margaret would continue to talk. Despite herself, Jessica couldn't help but be intrigued by this latest mystery. The dead man didn't seem to have any out and out enemies exactly, but it did appear as if he had upset people throughout his life. Could any one of them have decided to take ultimate action?

"I'm sure that folk are already saying that Desmond Wilcott and I were sworn enemies!" Margaret continued. "And it's true that we had our differences. He was a difficult, pernickety man, but that wisnae the issue – I've known plenty of difficult men like that. No, it was that I did not approve of the way he conducted his business. I did not approve at all. When he retired from the bank – well, I'd left the committee at that point, although I've always still entered and helped out at the Show. I'd never deny my help, of course. I just couldnae sit alongside him on the committee, not after what he'd done to my laddie and all those other members of staff who lost their jobs through no fault of their own at all. It just didnae seem fair, the way he retired on a big cushy bonus and a nice healthy pension, when so many folk had to leave the area and move to the city in the hopes of getting another job. No, it didnae seem right at all. Why should a hard-working lad like my Robert have to move away from home, and I'm hardly ever seeing him, when Desmond Wilcott gets to swan about on cruises and big long trips to Australia? No, if you ask me, he got what was coming to him."

Margaret Mustard uttered these last words almost to herself. She had seemed increasingly unaware of Jessica's presence as she spoke, her expression getting darker and more malevolent even as her voice got quieter and more deliberate. Jessica didn't say anything, not sure how to respond. She hadn't really thought that Margaret could have anything to do with Desmond Wilcott's death, but now she was not so sure.

Jessica was distracted by Ealisaid exiting the inner office. She left with just a wave, her footsteps clattering down the concrete stairs outside. Jessica knew that her friend wanted to be at the Show for the crowds arriving.

Murdo invited her to come through to the inner office next, and Jessica complied, taking a seat on the near side of Grant's large wooden desk. Margaret Mustard was left waiting in the outer office. Murdo re-took his seat next to DI Gordon on the other side of the desk and the interview began.

Jessica had experience of the police formalities, having been interviewed in a case earlier in the year, shortly after arriving in Dalkinchie for the first time. It didn't really lessen her nerves though, as being interviewed by the police was always a serious prospect.

"Miss Greer," said DI Gordon, "we have an idea of what took place in the judging room this morning, but we understand that you were also present at the judging of the cakes and preserves and would like your version of events. Can you tell us when you arrived at the Village Hall this morning?"

"I arrived at 8.30am. I went immediately to the cakes and preserves room. I wanted to observe the registration process, and Ealisaid...Miss Robertson was registering the jams and marmalades from 8.30 to nine. She was busy with a line of people when I arrived, and I looked around at the room, at the set-up and the rules on the wall."

"Can you tell us why you wanted to observe the process, Miss Greer?"

"I'm a junior reporter for *The Drummond and Dalkinchie Herald.* I've only been in Scotland a couple of months and I've never attended the Show before. I'm writing the main feature on it for *The Herald,* and Grant Mack, my editor, wanted me to have a full idea of how it worked."

"Thank you. Did you notice Margaret Mustard's marmalade being entered into the Show?"

"Yes. It was delivered by the MacNaughton and I...well, I was interested to see him in person. I haven't met him before."

DI Gordon nodded. Murdo interjected.

"Oh, the Laird's quite the character roond here, right enough! Cannae miss him, always in the kilt and that big beard and full head o' hair. I'm surprised you've no' met him already though,

Jessica! Wis he not at your aunt's opening party? You've never seen him in the café?"

Jessica was about to reply when she picked up on DI Gordon's impatient sideways look at Murdo. "There's no need to answer that Miss Greer. He is somewhat of a local celebrity, so it makes sense that your attention would be drawn to his entry. You didn't realise at the time that it was Margaret Mustard's marmalade?"

"Actually, I did. They spoke about it and later Ealisaid told me again when we were checking the entry numbers. I noticed the Castle Drummond label and Ealisaid explained that it was Margaret's marmalade."

Jessica faltered, not wanting to repeat the rest of her friend's words but realising that they may be significant, she continued: "She also said that technically the entry broke the rules, because the jar and the label weren't plain, but that Mr Wilcott never challenged it – he wouldn't do so because it was the MacNaughton that entered it. This was after registration had closed though. There was no-one else there."

"So Mrs Mustard's marmalade was the last entry?"

"No, there was another one before it closed. Donald Donaldson handed in a cake and some jam. On behalf of his wife, he said. Then everyone had entered so we closed the door, and that was when Ealisaid checked all the entry numbers before locking up. She left at that point, and I had a quick look in the main hall, then came here to work on my article at the desk out there."

"Hang on a minute , Miss Greer. You say that Ealisaid locked the door. What is your best estimate of the time that was?"

"It would be around 9.10 am. She went to the café to check on opening, and I went to the hall, then here."

Murdo interjected again.

"That would be about right, Sir! I was opening up the café for 9am with Mairead Robertson, Ealisaid's sister, and Ealisaid herself would have turned up aroond 9.15am. I mind because I'd just turned on the coffee grinder and I didnae hear her come in, but when I looked up, there she was."

DI Gordon looked contemplative. "Well, that's certainly consistent. Thank you. And you returned to the room...when?"

"At 11.30, although I was back at the Village Hall for eleven. I took more notes in the main hall. I wanted to see the crafts up close, without all the people in the way. It was judging time at that point. Magnus was there too, taking photos."

"Thank you, Miss Greer. It might be that we need to speak to yourself and to Mr Smith again to get more detailed information about who was present during your visits to the main hall, but that will suffice for now. Can you tell me, in your own words, what you observed when you attended the judging of the cakes and preserves?"

Jessica continued, describing as best she could the judging process and what she remembered of Mr Wilcott's behaviour up to the point where he collapsed. DI Gordon took detailed notes and nodded encouragingly from time to time. He asked her to repeat the information about the marmalade, and whether she was really sure that it had been the pot of Castle Drummond marmalade that was the last one tasted before Mr Wilcott's collapse. Jessica was very sure – there had been no mistaking the jar's distinctive curved shape, and the Castle Drummond label. She hoped that Margaret Mustard couldn't hear anything from the outside office. She didn't think she would be able to.

"Thank you, Miss Greer. You have been very helpful. You may now leave, and please send Mrs Mustard in."

Jessica nodded and stood up. In the outer office, Margaret Mustard was no longer looking as calm as she had earlier. In fact, she was looking positively ill again. Her colour was high, and her breath short. Perhaps it had not been a good idea to leave her interview until last. Clearly Margaret Mustard was not a woman who benefited from sitting in quiet contemplation.

Before Jessica could invite her to go in to the interview room, there came the noise of thudding footsteps from the stairs outside. All at once, there was a brisk knock at the door to the outer office, and then, without waiting for a reply, the door flew open and there stood the MacNaughton, resplendent in his kilt, standing with his balled hands on his hips – *like a Scottish Superman*, Jessica thought to herself. He went straight to Margaret Mustard who immediately stood up and burst into noisy sobs.

"Margaret! They telt me you were here. Are you OK, lass?"

"Oh, Gillespie! I'm all at sixes and sevens. There's a problem wi' my Show marmalade. They're even saying that Desmond Wilcott died after eating it! As if it had been poisoned! We were certainly no' friends, but I wouldnae do such a thing, not to my worst enemy!"

"Aye right, enough Margaret, calm down, calm down." Gillespie MacNaughton fished a clean cotton handkerchief square from his kilt sporran. Margaret Mustard took it and buried her face in it, sobbing noisily. The MacNaughton put his hands on her shoulders, muttering "there, there," as her sobs subsided to a noisy sniffle. There was something really touching about the way Gillespie MacNaughton was caring for Margaret, Jessica thought to herself.

The noise drew DI Gordon and Murdo from the inner office. Gillespie MacNaughton turned to them and said, in his deep, booming voice: "Can you explain yourselves? Why on earth would you need to haul a harmless wee lady up here for questioning? Can you no' tell she's not in a fit state to manage it?"

DI Gordon's tone was respectful, but he was direct in his reply.

"Mrs Mustard very kindly agreed to assist us with our enquiries earlier on, and she was not in distress then. Obviously we will take all the time she needs to calm down before proceeding. The fact remains, however, that a man has died suddenly, and the circumstances warrant investigation. A man who was in perfect health ingested a substance, and then immediately took ill, collapsed and died. We need to look into that substance and into anything else that might have happened before this took place."

"Ingested a substance? What on earth do you mean?"

Murdo spoke up.

"The marmalade, Chief – Mr Wilcott was judging the marmalade when he took no' weel. It seems likely it wis Mrs Mustard's marmalade, so we are just checking."

"Margaret's orange and whisky marmalade? The one I entered this morning?" The MacNaughton knitted his brows together in confusion, looked to the side and rubbed at his bearded chin. "But how could that be?"

"That's what we are trying to find out, Mr MacNaughton."

"No, I mean..." The MacNaughton looked at Margaret Mustard and shrugged. "Margaret, I'm going tae have tae come clean. I didnae register your Show marmalade."

He turned to DI Gordon and Murdo, as a bewildered expression spread over the faces of everyone present.

"Margaret always picks oot her Show jar, the one that she

thinks is best filled, the best colour and the neatest. She sets it aside in the pantry for me to register on the day. But I wis in a wee bit o' a hurry this morning, and I'm a bit clumsy anyway. When I picked up the jar it slipped out of my hand and it smashed on the floor. We've got flagstones, hard as concrete they are. I cleaned it all up, and you'd never know!"

"So when you registered my preserves..." Margaret Mustard spoke slowly, trying to comprehend.

"I just swapped in one o' the other jars. I made sure to pick the cleanest, neatest looking one! Not that most folk could tell any difference between them. She's a perfectionist," he added unnecessarily to the gathered group.

"So, if you think that Margaret – or anybody else for that matter – dropped a wee bit o' poison into her Show marmalade, then I'm glad to be able to tell you that you're mistaken! Quite apart from the fact that she would never do such a thing, the jar intended for the Show is back in the Drummond Castle bins."

The MacNaughton looked around, beaming in delight. It was evident that he felt he had exonerated Margaret. Murdo's face was serious, his expression concentrating. Jessica always found it hard to read DI Gordon's face but he too seemed to be working something out.

"How many other jars of marmalade were there, Mr Mac-Naughton?"

"Half a dozen or so. That would be about right, would it not, Margaret?"

Margaret Mustard, uncharacteristically silent, nodded. She didn't appear to be relieved by this new information, Jessica noted. In fact, quite the opposite – her expression was one of pure strain.

Surely this was good news – it showed that Margaret Mustard

had not poisoned the jar beforehand. What, then, could be causing her such stress?

6

McScunnered's Trail

There was a brief moment of silence. Then everyone began talking at the same time.

The MacNaughton, clearly not getting the reaction he had hoped for, started to repeat his story but more slowly and with more emphasis. "So I went to the pantry see, and I grabbed the first jar to put in the basket, and I don't know what I did but it just sort of jumped out of my hand and fell. It was like it wis in slow motion, a wee tumble tae the ground where it smashed and made a nice big sticky glass mess! So I cleared it all up then went to a different bit of the shelf where Margaret keeps the batches, and I got one from there..."

Murdo was wondering out loud: "but if you registered a different jar of marmalade...then it couldnae be the marmalade at all, could it? Or if it WIS the marmalade...then it would need to be tampered wi' in the judging room? Or is all the marmalade poisoned? Or maybe Mr Wilcott had an allergic reaction to something in the marmalade?"

Jessica, nervous for her friend, reiterated that Ealisaid had been in the room the entire time the marmalades were being registered and would have noticed anyone opening a jar. The door had been locked when the registration finished, and not re-opened again until the judging. She mused aloud whether the stewards would have noticed anything at that point.

Margaret, having found her voice, was mainly repeating again and again how she would never purposefully do such a thing, and anyone who knows her could vouch for that – she was well-known hereabouts.

The Detective Inspector, twisting his head from one speaker to the next, eventually gave up and said firmly, "I'm going to have to ask you all to be quiet. Please, give me a moment." His voice carried, and everyone stopped speaking. There was a moment of silence, then DI Gordon spoke again.

"Mr MacNaughton. The jar of marmalade that you entered into the Show was not the jar that Mrs Mustard had intended to enter. The original jar was broken."

"Spot on!"

"Mrs Mustard, you made several jars of marmalade in this batch and stored them all in the pantry at Castle Drummond."

"Yes, although I don't quite see – "

"Miss Greer, as far as you are aware, all the marmalade jars were entered into the Show in a single half hour period, after which the door to the room was locked. It was not reopened until the judging began."

"You got it."

"Then it seems we have ourselves a bit of a conundrum. We will need to await testing on the marmalade – it's the weekend, so I don't imagine we will have results before Monday. Mrs Mustard and Mr MacNaughton, I will still need to take short statements from you both but we will try not to keep you longer than necessary. Miss Greer, you are free to go but we will try to speak to you tomorrow for a more detailed breakdown of the people and timings you observed at the Show."

Jessica nodded, and left the office. It wasn't until she had reached the bottom of the stairs that she remembered about the anonymous letter-writer Mrs Wilcott had talked about. Should she have mentioned it to the police?

* * *

The Show had begun when Jessica entered, and she wandered around making a note of the prize winners. She knew she would receive a full, official list, but took some detailed notes on how to describe them. It was hard to know whether this Show was typical or not, given that it was her first. Certainly there was a sombre air hanging over the main hall. She couldn't see Ealisaid anywhere, but numerous signs informed Show attendees of the truncated nature of the event.

Moving down the middle aisle towards the woodwork class, Jessica ran into Grant Mack. He was alone, having persuaded his mother to stay at the café for a cup of tea while he checked out the situation. "It's fine though, Jessica - I think I will bring her up for half an hour or so. She'll be happy to see the knitting and she won't notice the lack of cakes. I made sure she had a slice of something delicious at *Lissa's.*"

Grant was an earnest man, with a serious demeanour. He was rangy, with frank brown eyes, a friendly face, and hair that flopped over his forehead. As his mother's main carer he was often accompanied by her, and it was unusual in the extreme to see him without his loyal black labrador, Skye. A patient beast, she had tolerated the puppy nonsense from young Willow on the couple of occasions the two had spent time together. Reenie and Grant had grown close since Reenie's arrival in Dalkinchie, and now spent some time together at least once per week.

Jessica was fond of her boss, who was in possession of a principled mind and a finely honed sense of fairness. He was also an excellent mentor, challenging her just the right amount so that Jessica could learn, while also teaching her real journalistic skills and everything he knew about living and working in the same small community. She trusted him. Before settling in to Dalkinchie, she had been uncertain about her future as a journalism student and her place at grad school. Although working on a small local Scottish newspaper had not exactly been one of her ambitions, she felt like it was turning out to be an excellent preparation for a future career.

"Grant, what should we do about the Show feature? I assumed I can't just write what we planned – it would be disrespectful. I have enough already, plus the winners, to write a pared down report, and I will attend the presentation and write that up too."

"I absolutely agree, Jessica, I had similar thoughts myself. I wondered whether it might be fitting to write up this year's Show as you have suggested, simple listing of the facts and figures, and use the rest of the space for a retrospective of all the Craft Shows during Desmond Wilcott's tenure as Show Convenor and head judge – perhaps picking out special entries, and particular events of note. I think that could work, but I'm afraid that it might involve quite a bit of research for you. Everything you need should be at the offices; I can show you how to access those old archived issues, but it's likely to involve some work tomorrow. Would that be a problem?"

"No problem at all. I'd planned to write tomorrow anyway. I can be at the offices all day. Actually, there's something else I'd quite like to research."

"Oh?"

"I sat with Mrs Wilcott for a little while before she went to the hospital. She told me about her husband and how he'd had this feud in the letters pages with someone – she didn't say who."

Grant nodded. "McScunnered."

"Excuse me?" Jessica wasn't sure she had heard him correctly. She knew that *scunnered* was a Scottish word meaning 'annoyed', but she had never heard it as a surname before.

"McScunnered. I know all about it. Mr Wilcott and an anonymous letter-writer calling themselves 'McScunnered' had entire conversations which played out in the letter pages. Do the police know about this?"

"Not from me. Mrs Wilcott might have mentioned it to them. I forgot, but I didn't really have any information about it anyway. Do you think it could be relevant?"

"Well, if you are looking up old issues anyway, you'll be bound to come across some of the correspondence and you can see for yourself. Some of the – *discussions* – got quite heated. I don't remember anything identifiable, but no harm in looking. It might come in handy."

"I will. What time should I come to the office tomorrow?"

"Shall we say 10.30? My mother will be at church with some of her friends. They come and pick her up. I'll show you the microfiche, and where I keep the limited hard copies. We will only be looking for August editions, and luckily the Show falls in the same week every year. It shouldn't take too long. We can make a rough outline as well."

Pleased with this plan, Jessica bid Grant goodbye and turned to leave the hall. She had enough material for now, and her heart was no longer in the events of the Show. Looking around for Ealisaid, she spotted that Donald Donaldson had entered the hall. He spotted her at the same moment, and – clearly recognising her – made his way across the room with a clear intention of speaking to her.

"Miss! Miss!"

"Hi, Mr...Donaldson isn't it?"

"Who can I speak to about retrieving my wife's cake stand? There is a sign on the door saying that the room is locked, and that no one can have access until tomorrow."

"That's correct, at least, you would probably be better speaking to Ealisaid, but I don't see her just now. However I do know that the room has to remain closed for the time being."

"Well, that's a terrible inconvenience I must say. That cake stand is a particularly fine one, and at previous shows I've always been able to take it back on the same day."

Jessica looked at the man in amazement. Could he really be so insensitive as to make a big deal about the cake stand now, when a man had died? A man who had apparently been his friend? Perhaps Donald Donaldson didn't have any other way of communicating. Perhaps he was so used to people listening to every word he had to say that the minute he met with any resistance this was the reaction.

"Mr Donaldson, I know you are aware of what happened earlier, and the death of Mr Wilcott. Unfortunately the room has to remain closed until that can be investigated further. After that, I'm sure the committee will make sure that everyone's belongings are returned to them as soon as possible."

The man backed down, a curious expression coming over his face. He rubbed his open hand over his large, florid face. When he next spoke, his words were less abrasive.

"Oh, yes...yes...a terrible affair. Terribly sad. Desmond Wilcott was a close personal friend, and he will be sadly missed, sadly missed. We have his wife in our home at the moment; she is extremely distressed as you might be able to imagine. We've had the doctor out."

Jessica found it hard to picture the scene. Everything she'd seen of Patricia Wilcott up until this point had displayed a woman with a calm, even temperament. She hadn't yet seen her in distress. Even upon receiving the news of her husband's death she had remained in control. In fact, the most agitated Jessica had seen her was when she had overheard her conversation about rebooking flight tickets to Australia.

"Of course, Desmond and his wife didn't always get along, sometimes things were famously frosty between them, but she is still very upset of course. I mean, Every relationship has its ups and downs, but perhaps theirs more than most. They just could not seem to agree on what best to do to support their daughter. Still, I suppose it's all water under the bridge now. We must move on. A terrible tragedy. Anyway, if you do see Ealisaid Robertson, please let her know that we will be back to pick up the cake stand tomorrow. And thank you for your help Miss – ?"

"Greer. Jessica Greer. I'm glad to have been able to help. I'm sorry for the loss of your friend."

Donald Donaldson nodded distractedly, then exited the Hall as quickly as he had come in. Jessica watched after him. Could the Wilcotts' strained relationship have more impact on this case than she had previously realized?

* * *

"And then he just left!" Curled up on one of Reenie's sofas, Jessica had just finished telling the whole story to Reenie, who was sitting on the floor trying to settle Willow on her puppy bed. Willow preferred cozying up on Reenie's feet – or Jessica's, or indeed anyone's who stayed still for long enough. Reenie was persevering with settling her in more appropriate locations, but Jessica secretly loved the warm weight of the puppy lying across her feet.

"Interesting," commented Reenie. "So, do you really think the Wilcott marriage was in trouble?"

Jessica shrugged. "I don't know. I'm certainly getting the idea that Desmond Wilcott was a difficult man, a strict man, perhaps someone who was hard to live with. But I'm not sure I can imagine that it went any further than that."

Reenie was quiet for a moment. She had given up trying to settle Willow, and was instead now playing with her, running her fingers across the wooden floor and causing the puppy to nose at, and then chase them. Willow let out a short playful bark and bounced backwards into a play bow, which made both women laugh.

"Tell me again about the marmalade – I'm still not sure I understand completely."

"The marmalade that Desmond Wilcott ate was not the one that Margaret Mustard had intended to enter into the Show. It doesn't exonerate her completely, but it does mean that she didn't put poison in one jar and enter it in the show. That's assuming it is poison," finished Jessica, aware that she was getting ahead of herself. There was no such evidence yet.

"The police are taking it pretty seriously, though," said Reenie, having successfully managed to get Willow to lie down on her dog bed for a few seconds.

"Yes. Yes, they are. They are definitely pursuing this line of enquiry. I don't know whether they perhaps know something that I don't, maybe some information from the hospital or his medical records. It does seem as if they believe there was something in the marmalade."

"And enemies are mounting up? People who have a problem with Desmond Wilcott?" Reenie said this enquiringly.

"Not exactly enemies, but quite a few people who maybe could have a grudge. There was a scandal at the bank where he worked, although he wasn't affected. I'm going to look into something tomorrow actually. Mrs Wilcott told me about a feud with a letter writer, and Grant says I will see this for myself in old editions of the newspaper. I'm speaking to the police again later on tomorrow too, and if they think it's useful I might end up investigating it more."

"Well, just you look out for yourself, Jessica." Reenie always took her role *in loco parentis* seriously, and sometimes spoke to Jessica like a child. "I know you enjoy this type of mystery, and you certainly have a flair for it. But if somebody did intentionally poison Desmond Wilcott, then they probably won't take too kindly to you looking into it. Particularly when one of the people is anonymous, and you won't know who it is until possibly it's too late."

"I'll be careful," said Jessica. "At the moment it's just doing some research in old newspapers, which I have to do anyway to put together a feature on the Show. No one will know what I'm really doing. I'll pass on anything I find to the police immediately – if they want me to, that is."

Reenie nodded, evidently reassured. Jessica took the opportunity to ask her aunt for some further advice.

"Reenie...I've been wondering about visiting Mrs Wilcott. I sat with her for a while before she got the news about husband, and I think she would appreciate the company. Would that be appropriate do you think?"

Reenie's response came immediately. "Yes, I think that would be fine. The poor woman is probably feeling incredibly lonely. If you like I can give you a gift from the shop – not cut flowers, I always find it too complicated to deal with at times like this, perhaps a nice flowering plant. I'll find the perfect thing for you."

"Thank you, that would be great. I might try and go tomorrow evening. I think Ealisaid might come too, and she'll probably take some food."

"That's a good idea, too. One less thing for Mrs Wilcott to think about. So that would be the evening? You are working tomorrow during the day?"

"Yes. I'm meeting Grant at 10.30."

"I hope you have fun. I am going to enjoy my one day off." Reenie yawned and put her feet up.

* * *

Jessica watched Grant as he methodically showed her how to use the sturdy microform reader in the corner. She had never used one before – the college she attended had had an extensive digital library but nothing on microfilm or microfiche. *The Herald's* back issues were held on microfiche, flat sheets of film stored in papery archival envelopes. Secretly relieved, because the lack of film meant that she wouldn't have to spool the roll on to the feeder, Jessica watched as Grant loaded the sheet carefully on to the glass, moved it under the light and demonstrated the manual zoom, focus and rotate functions. He then stepped aside for her to have a try. Jessica followed the instructions exactly, holding the fiche delicately by the edges as she transferred it to the plate, and took hold of the dials herself.

Grant smiled at her seriousness. "We thought this was the future, we really did. The space saved was amazing. All those bundles of newspapers, reduced to a tiny little stack of envelopes. Now, of course, we have all this microfiche film that we have to keep relatively stable, and meanwhile the readers are slowly breaking down. I don't even think they can be repaired any more, certainly there's no maintenance contract. I'm sure there's an up-to-date reader, or something that will convert them all to another digital form for us but strangely, local Scottish newspaper archives don't seem to be much of a funding priority. Maybe one day I'll do a fundraiser, try and bring some money in to get it done. Not right now, though." Grant passed a hand over his furrowed brow and, not for the first time, Jessica wondered how he managed to get everything done. Perhaps the digitization project could be something she could take on during her year in Dalkinchie.

Grant then explained the filing system, which was organised chronologically by year and month. "We should definitely have all the issues covering Desmond Wilcott's tenure as Show Convenor. I'm less sure that we will have a complete run of letter pages. I have a feeling that they weren't considered high priority at the outset, but I'm sure at some point that they were converted to microfiche too. Anything we don't have is available in the City Archives in Dundee. They have more on film, and also an extensive collection of hard copies. However, that's probably getting ahead of ourselves. Focus on the Show for now, and if the police make the identity of McScunnered a priority, we will tackle that then."

Jessica nodded. Grant bid his farewell and left, leaving her to the research.

* * *

By the time DI Gordon and Murdo arrived at the office, Jessica had found plenty of material for her tribute Show article. As Grant had suggested, it had been really simple to find the relevant issues as the Show took place in the same weekend in August every year, and had done since approximately the dawn of time. Desmond Wilcott had run thirteen Shows as Convenor, and Jessica had been able to find the write-up of his first Show, as well as picking out highlights from many events across the years. With the results of this year's Show, she was confident she could put together an article that not only contained the information people would be looking for this year, but also honored Desmond Wilcott's service to the Craft Show. She only hoped that she could do this tastefully. With that accomplished, she had moved on to the task of finding out as much as she could about the intriguingly named McScunnered. She worked backwards, first looking at the letter pages in the Show issues of the newspaper, and then expanding her search. What she had found convinced her it was worth mentioning to the police. She was sure that they would be interested.

"Dear Sir,

I refer to last week's letter offered by your anonymous correspondent who prefers to go by the pseudonym 'McScunnered.' Once again, I am convinced that his choice to use an epithet is due to embarrassment at an evident lack of education. The case presented is simply inaccurate, and one wonders what McScunnered stands to gain from presenting it. Perhaps if we had a sense of his true identity, this self-interest would be revealed. As it is, surely his opinions are best ignored, and I question their inclusion in your paper.

Yours, etc,

Desmond Wilcott."

Jessica, agog, found the reply printed a week later.

"Dear Sir,

Mr Wilcott does not like opinions contrary to his own, and once again, his suggested solution is censorship. Unfortunately he will find that he is not the only person to have a voice in the community, and that the free press will not allow his the sole opinion to be aired. He no doubt enjoyed such privilege in his professional life! Perhaps Mr Wilcott would be surprised at the local strength of feeling on this matter. Surely public facilities should be decided on by the public, and not by a single individual who appears bent upon a dictatorship?

Yours sincerely,

McScunnered of Drummond."

This entire exchange seemed to be related to a change in opening hours and management of the local public restrooms near the park. Reading back, Jessica came across many similar exchanges over the years, all of them related to apparently trivial local matters. Grant had explained that the previous editor had gone with an open publication policy and he had followed suit, publishing every letter sent in, so that no letter-writer could accuse the newspaper of bias. This led to long-running spats, taking place over weeks and weeks in *The Herald's* pages, often with no reference to the original disagreement.

Desmond Wilcott always signed off with his name in full, and his adversary with 'McScunnered' or 'McScunnered of

Drummond'. Apart from that there was no clue as to the identity of the letter-writer, and although Jessica noted that Desmond Wilcott had clearly thought he was arguing with a man, she found nothing among the letters she read which indicated that this was definitely the case. The letter that convinced her that it was worth raising with the police read as follows:

"Dear Sir,

Mr Wilcott has shown himself to be quite ruthless in local matters, often ignoring or discarding the hard work of others in his pursuit of leadership. While this seemed to have served him well in the workplace, he is not the gaffer any more and he will soon find out that it's not an attitude he can take for long as a member of the community without repercussions.

Yours sincerely,

McScunnered of Drummond."

Jessica moved the plate, reading this letter over several times. Given recent events, it distinctly read as a threat.

Had McScunnered followed through with the repercussions?

7

A Visit to Drummond

J essica was still poring over the letters when DI Gordon and Murdo arrived. They wanted a better sense of who had been around at the Village Hall in the morning before the Show had opened and had already spoken to Magnus, hoping that his time-stamped photographs would give a clearer picture. Unfortunately Magnus had zoomed in to get close-ups of the crafts, and had deliberately avoided having any people in the background, so his memory was all they had to go on.

Jessica didn't fare much better. Apart from the groups of judges, and the people she had seen setting up their crafts – all of whom were documented on Show administration lists – she couldn't remember the exact timings and details of any specific person who had been there in the Hall. She remembered the Wilcotts' arrival very clearly, but that was it. The Detective Inspector seemed quite resigned. There was a lot of information to sift through, and Jessica didn't envy the challenge of narrowing it down. She spoke up:

"DI Gordon, there is some information you might find helpful. Mrs Wilcott mentioned that her husband had a feud with someone in *The Herald* letter pages, and I've managed to find quite a lot of them, including one I think you should look at. It's still on the reader." Jessica gestured to the microfiche reader in the corner. DI Gordon followed her lead, sitting down in front of the clunky machine and adjusting the focus until he was comfortable. Jessica noticed that he didn't have to be shown how to use it. He peered closely at the screen.

"Can you show me any of Mr Wilcott's letters?"

Jessica nodded, moving the fiche off the plate and adding in the previous week's issue. DI Gordon read it in a contemplative silence. He then switched the fiche again to re-read the threatening letter.

"Who is this McScunnered? Constable Smith, does this ring any bells?"

"No' really, although I might have heard the name mentioned. I don't really read the letters pages in the paper. McScunnered? That's a made-up name, surely? There's nobody roond here wi' a name like that! Can you imagine being landed wi' 'scunnered' in your name, you'd be permanently annoyed."

Murdo gave a wide smile at Jessica who smiled back. Murdo always had a way of making a situation seem lighter.

"Indeed, this writer does seem to be annoyed. Perhaps that's why they chose this particular pseudonym. There are a lot of these letters, Miss Greer?"

"Yes, going back for years. That was the most threatening one I found, although I didn't check all the records we have. Plus, the letters are missing for some of the earlier editions, although Grant did say that they would be available in Dundee."

"Yes, of course. Was there anything identifying on any of the letters? Anything that might give more of a clue as to who exactly McScunnered might be?"

"Not that I found so far. I can keep looking if you like?" Jessica relished the research task. Now that she had mastered the microfiche, she was enjoying looking through back issues of the newspaper – as well as an interesting investigative challenge, it was also fascinating to see the evolution of local news over the last decade. She could feel her understanding of journalism deepen, looking at the scale and frequency of stories that appeared in the local newspaper over time.

"If you have time, that would be extremely useful Miss Greer, thank you. I will give you my number, and can you let me know if you find anything by the end of the day? If not, I think a trip to Dundee might well be on the cards. We have to start somewhere."

DI Gordon looked grimly off into the middle distance, no doubt contemplating the enormity of the task before him. A hall full of people, freely moving in and out. A pot of marmalade in a locked room, but to which many people could have had access either before or after its entry into the Craft Show. And Desmond Wilcott, whose actions in life increasingly appeared to show him to have been a very unpleasant man.

Jessica wondered again whether she should tell the police the conversation she had overheard from Mrs Wilcott, and decided against it. Her feelings of sympathy for the victim's wife were only increasing as time went on.

Perhaps after visiting she would feel differently.

* * *

Ealisaid turned up at Reenie's cottage that evening, exactly as promised. She drove an old car that had belonged to her mother, a dilapidated blue Beetle which Jessica had never ridden in before. She got in gingerly, although so far it felt more sound than the shuddering old green van that Reenie had been driving around in for over a decade. Jessica felt that any suspension that old clunker had ever had had been rattled away over Edinburgh cobblestones. The Beetle felt like a positively smooth ride by comparison.

On the back seat lay a casserole dish with the lid wedged on tightly, and a tub which Jessica was sure would be full of some deliciously tempting sweet treats. She herself clutched a potted flowering plant. Reenie had gone to her shop earlier that day especially to pick one out for her and had ended up choosing a pretty red kalanchoe which she'd assured Jessica wouldn't need much ongoing care, and would therefore be a perfect gift.

Ealisaid knew where the Wilcott house was, having attended Craft Show committee meetings there before. It was a few miles away from Dalkinchie in the neighbouring town of Drummond, where the MacNaughton also resided in Castle Drummond upon the hill.

They drew up and parked on the street outside; a white Volkswagen Golf occupied the driveway of the attractive detached stone house. It was set in large landscaped gardens and Jessica marveled at the views it would command – over the hills and down the glen towards Dalkinchie. She wondered briefly if Mrs Wilcott would be at home, as Donald Donaldson had said she was staying with them the day before, but she needn't have worried. Patricia Wilcott answered the door herself, looking tired but composed, and as neatly turned out as the day before.

"Jessica, hello. And Ealisaid. How kind of you to come by. Please, do come in. Donald is here, but I think he's just about to leave."

Jessica was bolstered by this welcome, and felt more convinced she had done the right thing by visiting. Patricia took the plant from Jessica and the cake tin from Ealisaid, but the latter insisted on carrying the heavy casserole through to the kitchen with her. Jessica was directed to the sitting room which lay to the left just inside the front door. It was a large airy room, furnished in soothing pale greens with papered walls, a plush carpet under Jessica's feet and solid, dark wood furniture including a piano in one corner of the room. The top of the piano was covered with framed photographs, mostly of a girl with long dark hair who Jessica assumed to be the Wilcott's daughter. In one she was holding a baby, and beaming at the camera.

Donald Donaldson was indeed present, standing with his back to the door, in front of a long mantelpiece above an elegant tiled fireplace. The shelf was laden with trophies and shields, all highly polished and reflecting the August sun which was slanting through the large picture window as it set; she had not been wrong about the views over the hills.

Donald Donaldson turned around briefly as Jessica entered the room.

"Hello again. I didn't know you were a friend of Patricia's. We have not been properly introduced. I'm Donald Donaldson."

Jessica replied hesitantly. Did he not remember that he had been quite rude to her on the two previous occasions they had met?

"I'm Jessica Greer, I have been in Dalkinchie for a couple of months. I'm a friend of Ealisaid's who is here too, and I was present yesterday when…when Mrs Wilcott received her sad news. I just wanted to come over and pay my respects."

Donald Donaldson nodded, and turning on his heel, began to pace back and forth. With his back to Jessica, he spoke.

"It's a terrible state of affairs. Just a dreadful thing to have to deal with. No matter what's going on between a husband and wife, when something like this happens it really knocks you for six. And it seems terribly likely that it was the marmalade! Who would believe it. The famous Castle Drummond Orange and Whisky. Why, I had some myself this morning."

His hands clasped behind his back, he quarter-turned towards Jessica and gave a small, sad closed mouth smile, then strolled to the centre of the mantelpiece where he seemed to be looking at a medium sized double-handed cup, placed to great effect in the centre of the display. He spoke again. "Despite everything, Patricia seems to be coping remarkably well. She was distressed yesterday yes, but she stayed with us and today she's very calm...very calm indeed. Determined to carry on as normal. I almost wonder..."

Whatever Donald Donaldson wondered, he didn't finish the thought. He picked up the cup, gently easing it from its crowded position without disturbing its neighbors, and held it up to the sunlight filtering through the window. The polished surface caught the fading beams and bounced them around the room as he turned it this way and that.

Patricia and Ealisaid entered the room, the former still thanking the latter for the casserole. As they did so, Donald Donaldson returned the cup to its position on the mantelpiece.

"No need to return the dish any time soon. If you like, I'll pop over in a week or so and pick it up. I'll let you know."

Patricia Wilcott thanked Ealisaid again. Donald Donaldson cleared his throat.

"If that's you settled in then Patricia, I'll be on my way. If you need anything, just let us know. Mary will pop in tomorrow and check how things are. There's no need to see me out, I'll let you attend to your...visitors."

"Thank you for everything, Donald, and do pass on my gratitude to Mary as well. You have both been so kind. I think I will be OK now, but if anything crops up I'll be sure to let you know, and I'll keep you updated with developments."

Donald Donaldson departed, with a nod in both Jessica and Ealisaid's direction. Jessica heard the front door close behind him and watched as the white Golf started up, pulled out of the drive and disappeared into the distance.

"Can I get you both a cup of tea? It would be no trouble."

Jessica didn't know whether it would be better to accept or decline, and was grateful when Ealisaid replied. "Tea would be lovely, but let me make it. You've been through a lot this weekend."

"I'll let you help, Ealisaid, but it's a relief to be able to move around again. Donald and Mary mean well and they are very kind, but I've been treated like an invalid the whole time I was with them. Waited on hand and foot, barely allowed to stand up...they even called the doctor out who gave me a Valium. I wasn't going to take it, but I did get a good night's sleep which may not have happened otherwise. Let's make the tea together."

The two women moved through to the kitchen together, once again leaving Jessica in the sitting room. Unable to suppress her curiosity, she moved to the mantelpiece where she, too, looked at the cup that Donald Donaldson had been examining so closely. Like him, she lifted it gently from its place in order to rotate it and better read the engraved inscription.

Drummond Golf Club
Donaldson Memorial Cup
Awarded to Desmond Wilcott

Moving along the mantelpiece, Jessica could see that a

considerable percentage of the trophies were similar awards for golfing competitions. A couple of them, positioned at the back with their inscriptions slightly obscured, had been awarded to Patricia Wilcott for her lace work at the Dalkinchie Craft Show.

Her observations were interrupted by Patricia and Ealisaid arriving back. Ealisaid carried a tray, and Patricia had removed the plant from its wrapping and now placed it on the windowsill. She then hurried to pull out a small occasional table from a nest of tables stacked against the wall. She positioned it in front of the large sofa and Ealisaid placed the tray down. It held a large blue-and-white patterned porcelain tea pot, a matching milk jug and sugar bowl, and three fine bone china mugs. These were decorated with Scots words and their definitions, with Patricia keeping 'Wheesht', Ealisaid taking 'Stoater' and Jessica ending up with 'Blether'. Patricia had placed Ealisaid's millionaire shortbread on a plate and Jessica took a piece, along with a napkin from a small stack thoughtfully provided. Ealisaid's shortbread was exquisite, but crumbly.

"Thank you again for coming to visit, girls. You have shown such kindness over the past couple of days."

"I just wanted to see if you were OK. I mean, I know you can't..." Jessica trailed off, aware that her words were clumsy but not knowing the best way of expressing herself. Luckily Patricia seemed to understand her faltering sentiments.

"I think I am, as much as I can be. It was a terrible shock indeed, and the ongoing investigation is horrible, but I feel calm enough at the moment. Of course, that may change as I have to make arrangements, but right now I am not going to worry about any of that. I certainly appreciate not having to think about cooking, so thank you Ealisaid, and the plant is beautiful, Jessica – a little color around the place. Desmond had terrible hayfever so we never had cut flowers, and most plants seemed to disagree with him too."

She looked over at the plant and smiled. Jessica glanced at Ealisaid, whose face was impassive. Once again, Jessica felt a sense of unreality and eerie calm. She had no idea how a person who had just lost her husband was supposed to react, but this certainly seemed unusual. She remember Donald Donaldson's earlier words, and his statement yesterday about the Wilcott's marriage. Could Patricia even be happy that her husband was dead? It wasn't exactly a question she could ask!

"How is your daughter coping, Patricia?" Ealisaid asked. A shadow crossed Patricia Wilcott's face, and her tone was sorrowful when she spoke.

"I haven't actually told her yet. She's in Brisbane, Australia and the time zone – yesterday, by the time I would have been able to reach her I was asleep, knocked out by that stupid Valium. The best time is late evening here which is morning over there. I plan on speaking to her tonight. She and her father…well they didn't always get on, fathers and daughters you know – they clashed, mostly over money. She will be terribly upset though. I hope to see her soon."

"Yes, of course, she'll want to come over," Ealisaid nodded as she spoke but Jessica noticed that Patricia Wilcott didn't respond at all and wondered if she had, in fact, meant something entirely different – if, as the overheard phone call had suggested, Patricia was planning to travel to see her daughter, rather than the other way around.

Jessica changed the subject. "I was admiring your trophies on the shelf earlier. Mr Wilcott was really good at golf! There are so many!"

Patricia smiled. "Yes, he was. I barely noticed when he retired, as he switched from going to the office to spending at least as much time at the Golf Club. It was good for him to have a hobby, and Donald certainly enjoyed the fact that Desmond had more free time. I don't think he always enjoyed Desmond being the victor though, but that was Desmond all over – whatever he did, he had to excel. It was the source of the aggravation with our daughter as well. He was a pushy man. He pushed himself, and he pushed others too. When it came to golf, he's applied himself rigorously to it over the last few years and it paid off. He got better and better, winning almost everything lately, as you can see." She waved her hand at the array on the mantel. "Donald will miss him greatly. They've been golf partners for years."

The three women drank their tea in silence for a few moments. As fond as she was becoming of Patricia Wilcott, Jessica couldn't quiet the little voice running through her head: would Patricia miss her husband too?

Ealisaid and Jessica made further small talk as they finished up their tea, and then made moves to go, not wanting to tire Patricia or to keep her from her conversation with her daughter. As they left, another guest arrived to see her, a woman with short silvery curls and a distinctive long, patterned green raincoat. Patricia greeted her delightedly, clearly a close friend. Jessica dismissed her previous thoughts. Her first impression was surely correct, Patricia Wilcott was a pleasant woman who had a sometimes difficult relationship with a somewhat overbearing husband. That was quite common.

It certainly didn't make her a murderer.

8

Ye Banks and Braes o' Bonnie Tay

Monday found Jessica on the train to Dundee, accompanied by Murdo. Further research in the newspaper archives the day before had not unearthed any more clues as to the true identity of McScunnered, and, in the absence of any other potential leads, DI Gordon had sanctioned this trip. Grant was calling his contact at the City Archives as they traveled, and had given Jessica directions on how to find the building. Dundee wasn't a large city and it was all walkable, he had advised, most of it through the city centre past a small shopping centre – *mall*, Jessica had translated in her head – and other shops and restaurants.

The journey had been a multi-stage one. First Reenie had dropped them at the bus stop in Drummond, the three of them squeezing into the large front seat of her old green van, 'Susie'. From there they had caught a bus to a nearby train station on the Dundee line. Lastly, the train journey which, to Jessica's surprise, was on a comfortable, modern train complete with wifi and charging stations. It made its way steadily through the countryside, allowing Jessica a good view of the rolling hills, wide expanses of fields, now mostly harvested, and small towns along the way.

As they approached Dundee the train's speed slackened as it began to cross a long, curved rail bridge across a wide, sparkling river. "This'll be the Tay Bridge!" Murdo, looking out of the window, commented.

Of course. Jessica put two and two together. While studying poetry in her English literature major, the work of the Scottish poet William McGonagall had been discussed a few times as an example of doggerel, poetry that was poorly structured and rhymed. One of his more famous poems was 'The Tay Bridge Disaster.' Jessica could only remember the first few lines:

Beautiful railway bridge of the silv'ry Tay
Alas! I am very sorry to say
That ninety lives have been taken away

Their poetry professor had been at pains to point out the lazy rhyming, the lack of scansion and the inappropriate use of imagery in McGonagall's work, but Jessica, ever fascinated by Scotland due to her family connections, had hung on phrases such as 'silv'ry Tay' and 'Nearby Dundee and the Magdalen Green' and wondered whether she would ever get the chance to see them for herself. Now, that question was being answered.

As the train rounded the bridge into Dundee and Jessica looked at the silv'ry Tay herself, she felt her excitement rise at the chance to explore a new place. She hadn't left Dalkinchie and Drummond since her arrival in Scotland two months before, and a trip to the city might be just what she needed.

The train rolled into the station and Jessica and Murdo disembarked. The train station wasn't particularly large, but Jessica had the impression of industry and business. She realised suddenly that as it was the middle of August, the school holidays had ended, earlier than they would back at home in the U.S, and it was odd how she could almost feel the change in the air – a perceptible shift as the country moved from vacation back to routines, and to business as usual. It was 10 in the morning so they had missed the commuter rush, but the station was still full of people in office wear, as well as a few who were clearly tourists.

Exiting the railway station, Jessica looked back towards the river that they had just crossed by bridge. She knew that they had to head away from it towards the centre of the city, but she was interested in the new riverside developments that Grant had described. The *RRS Discovery,* famous as Captain Scott's Antarctic explorer vessel, had been docked in Dundee for decades, and now formed a visitor attraction. Reenie had mentioned herself and her twin Bella, Jessica's mom, visiting in their teens.

Adjacent to Discovery Point was a new and exciting building, a contemporary design for a new gallery that stood proudly on the circumference of the city, looking out over the Tay. The gallery was part of the Victoria and Albert collection of museums and galleries, and the first in Scotland. Jessica had read that the V&A, as it was affectionately known, housed a permanent collection of Scottish iconic design and also ran exhibitions focusing on different aspects of design history. The building was certainly imposing, formed of two conjoined roughly triangular buildings sitting on their apexes and rising in a jagged sweep towards a flat roof under the open sky. Today, another dry, bright day, it was visually impressive and its outline seemed to Jessica to echo the masts of the stalwart ship beside it. She hoped she and Murdo would be able to pay a short visit before catching the train on their return journey.

Grant had given Jessica sketchy directions to the City Archives and she was relying on the map on her cell phone for the rest. Murdo, not a frequent city visitor, was happy to leave navigation up to her. "Aye, I've been here before, but no' for years Jessica. I wouldnae be able to find anything at a'. I went to an agricultural show but it wisnae in the city centre...I cannae quite remember where it wis but it wis a great day. Pipes playin', and there wis a beer tent. I mind Magnus got intae trouble for samplin' the beer that day." Murdo chuckled to himself at the memory.

As keen as Jessica was to learn about the exploits of a younger Magnus, she knew she would have to concentrate to find their destination. "Grant said we should take a shortcut through an old graveyard. I think he thought it would save time and I would quite like it too. I like reading the inscriptions and I find graveyards peaceful. Are you cool with that? It's got a funny name – the Huff?"

"Oh aye, the Howff. I've heard of that. It dates from Mary, Queen o' Scots. Dinnae mind me, Jessica, I'm happy anywhere. It would maybe be quite interesting, being so old."

Jessica was getting used to Murdo's seemingly endless hive of knowledge. On the face of it he seemed to be entirely focused on farming and the rural community life, but occasionally he produced interesting facts or startling insights. This information about the Howff convinced her. Who didn't love the romanticism of poor, doomed Queen Mary? Plus, the Howff had appeared on her map and it was therefore a practical move to aim there first.

Around ten minutes later, Jessica and Murdo edged in through a small gate in the corner of the graveyard. According to the map, this was not the main entrance through which they would exit. The graveyard was not as large and imposing as Jessica had expected, thinking that a landmark like this would be grandiose. Instead the smallish patch of ground was very green, both with grassy patches and the dipping foliage of several perimeter trees, but gave the impression of being squeezed in between various high grey buildings. The rows of gravestones were close together and somewhat haphazardly arranged. A cobbled path lined with benches ran around and between the graves, some of which Jessica could see were extremely ornate. She and Murdo drifted slowly, pausing to read the inscriptions in a companionable silence.

It was peaceful; not another soul had decided to take the shortcut at this moment. The buzz of the city ebbed away as Jessica and Murdo reached the middle of the plot. They passed three stone sarcophagi and a stone table, which stood out as unusual amongst the standing gravestones and smaller monuments. Jessica found herself thinking of Aslan, and the ancient magic of the Narnian stone table in one of her favourite childhood books, *The Lion, The Witch and The Wardrobe.* Apart from the stone table, nothing else on this dry, fine August day was particularly Narnian.

She changed her mind a few minutes later when they left through the main entrance. Above it sat a stone heraldic crest, the crest itself displaying an urn with three flowers above it and buttressed on either side by a dragon-like creature, wings folded back. There was something inscribed above it but Jessica couldn't make out what it said, and in all likelihood it would have been in Latin anyway. She resolved to ask Grant later. They were only a couple of minutes from the City Archives now, and she hoped he had managed to speak to his contact there, and that they would be expected.

Indeed he had. Dr Ferguson, a short twinkly man wearing a buttoned up cardigan, welcomed them warmly. "Miss Greer, Mr Smith - welcome to Dundee City Archives. I've had a lovely chat this morning with my old friend Grant Mack about your visit. I understand you are in a bit of a hurry, so I will show you straight to the local newspapers section, but if you were ever able to come back I would be delighted to show you more of our collection. Miss Greer, I understand that you are working as a reporter for *The Drummond and Dalkinchie Herald?* And Mr Smith, you are a local farmer as well as your role in the constabulary?"

They kept up the conversation as they moved across the polished floors of the building. The long corridors were panelled with a rich wood, and above that were ornately framed portraits of solemn looking men, many in uniform. Jessica didn't get a chance to look at the small signs underneath each portrait to work out who they were, but she assumed them to be Dundee dignitaries and people of importance.

Dr Ferguson got them set up in a small private reading room, adjacent to the stacks and shelves of records. He left them with a smile and the promise of a cup of tea afterwards – no food or drink was permitted near the archives – and the support of a Records Officer who had been assigned to find the correct back editions of *The Herald* plus anything else that might be of use. Jessica had made a note of those that she had already been able to check, and Murdo was able to pinpoint the year in which the Wilcotts had arrived in Drummond. They decided to check the issues for a couple of years before that, just in case McScunnered had already been in the habit of writing in to the newspaper – or arguing with anyone else.

The officer provided more sheets of microfiche; there was a reader in the room, as well as some hard copy issues and archive boxes containing files of correspondence. The newspapers were delicate and they had been advised that they should only check those if they really felt that there was anything missing from the run on microfiche.

Jessica and Murdo divided the work, Jessica using the reader to check old letters pages and Murdo flicking through the hard copy correspondence in case there was anything from McScunnered that would give more of a clue to his, or her, identity. They worked steadily for over an hour, then were interrupted by Murdo's cell phone ringing. He left the building to take the call and while he was away Jessica worked on. Upon his return, he filled her in. Jessica was never sure whether he was meant to tell her information or not, but it didn't trouble Murdo.

"Jessica, that wis the Detective Inspector. They've had the test results back on the marmalade. There wis poison in the jar at the Show."

Jessica felt a sudden lurch in her stomach at his words. She wasn't sure why she felt so shocked. She'd known that this was suspected, otherwise why would she and Murdo be in Dundee, looking into the background of someone that might have had a motive against Desmond Wilcott? It had been clear to her that DI Gordon hadn't been sharing every piece of information he held, but that something about the case and Desmond Wilcott's death had strongly indicated foul play.

Now it was confirmed. The marmalade – Margaret Mustard's prized Castle Drummond Orange and Whisky Marmalade – had been poisoned all along.

"Do they know what kind of poison?"

"Aye, he said. It wis nicotine apparently, I didnae even know that it wis a poison that could be used like that. It causes heart failure if you take enough o' it, and the DI said that it was a fair amount. It disnae always kill you though – Mr Wilcott wis unlucky there. Sometimes it just makes you very ill."

Jessica reflected on his words. Nicotine, in the marmalade. That sounded very intentional – hardly something that could happen by accident. It definitely seemed as if someone had targeted Desmond Wilcott.

"There's something else – the poison wis only in the top layer of the marmalade, not mixed throughout the whole jar. A big dose, right at the tap."

"So that means – "

"No much, really. DI Gordon wis clear on that. He says…he said it doesn't *eliminate* the possibility that the poison was added at the Castle before the Show, it just strongly *indicates* that it wis poisoned later. Which means that it could have been a number of people. Anyone wi' access."

"I know, Murdo, but no-one had access, remember? Ealisaid locked the door after registration and opened up for the judging."

"Aye. The DI is headed to the Hall right now. He says to meet him there later, if we are back in time. He's going to find oot how many sets of keys there are. Oh and by the way, Jessica, dinnae tell anyone about the details about the poison in the marmalade. I've just remembered that the Detective Inspector said no' to tell anyone. I didnae think that meant you, but just in case – keep it to yourself, will you?"

Getting back to work, Jessica and Murdo swapped tasks for a while. She had found plenty more of the sorts of letter Desmond Wilcott and McScunnered had enjoyed exchanging, with various levels of heatedness and spite, but nothing that served as an outright threat or identified McScunnered. Her eyes were getting tired of looking at the illuminated transparencies and she decided that flicking through the boxes might rest them.

When she found it, at first she didn't realise what she was holding. On the face of it it just looked like the hard copy of a letter that she had already read on microfiche. Murdo had already found a couple of such letters and they had compared them with the printed versions. Occasionally the editor had cut down a phrase or used an abbreviation to save space, but there had been no significant insight. Until now.

"Dear Sir,

I refer to the letter from Mr D. Wilcott in your most recent issue, concerning the development of a local fund for community gardening projects. Mr Wilcott suggests that the administration of such a fund would be best managed by himself as a *de facto* treasurer of the group. I suggest that the community might wish to examine his track record with managing money and think twice before allowing this appointment. After all, the last thing that is required is any more mismanagement – not to mention corruption!

Yours faithfully,

McScunnered of Drummond."

Jessica remembered the letter. She had read it over a few times, because this one in particular seemed to be quite risky in its language. Could you outright accuse a person of being corrupt in a public forum and get away with it? Especially when it discussed finance, and Desmond Wilcott had worked in a bank! Upon re-reading, she realised that McScunnered had worded it quite cleverly – it only contained suggestion, and no direct accusation. Still, McScunnered, whoever it was, seemed a braver person than Jessica would be. At home, there was no way that her lawyer mom would have let this pass.

The previous letters from McScunnered that Murdo had found were word processed and printed on standard white printer paper. This was on a thicker parchment style paper, smaller with a slight creamy hue to it – and, Jessica noticed now, actually typewritten. The lettering had that slightly uneven, idiosyncratic look to it that betrayed it having been typed on a manual typewriter. For a moment Jessica briefly, wildly, considered that they might be able to find the typewriter and match the lettering to it, just as happened so frequently in the old British mysteries she had loved reading in her early teens. Then she realised that she was being ridiculous. This had to be so old that the typewriter would be long gone by now. She was holding the letter in her left hand by the top left corner so as not to handle it too much. She turned to Murdo and as she did so, she transferred the document to her other hand.

"Look, Murdo! This is another McScunnered letter and it's a little bit different."

"Oh, aye?" Murdo turned away from the screen, interested.

"It's…" Jessica glanced at the letter again and realised something else. Her thumb had been obscuring a small logo or monograph in the top left corner, and switching to her other hand had revealed it. She held it closer. It was an encircled pen and ink sketch, printed in a faded blood-red ink onto the creamy writing paper. It looked like the outline of a farmhouse. *Personalized stationery*. There was something else too, a couple of tiny words underneath the sketch. She moved it even closer and squinted at it.

Abbotsford Farm, Drummond, Jessica read.

* * *

The discovery of the letter and Murdo's instructions from the Detective Inspector meant that there was no time to linger in Dundee as Jessica had hoped to do. They completed the same journey in reverse and, back in Dalkinchie, Jessica and Murdo found DI Gordon still at the Village Hall.

Although the Show prize-giving and presentation on Saturday had been a relatively subdued affair, the two days of sales that had followed had gone ahead and attracted the usual healthy footfall. Ealisaid has told Jessica that the Show was marketed year-round online and in specialist print media, with the campaigns ramping up over the summer. It was one of the best places in Scotland to find examples of fine handmade authentic Scottish crafts, and was attended by not just members of the public, but by interested potential stockists, owners of businesses that provided accommodation, and wholesalers too. At 2.30pm on Monday afternoon, it still had a couple of hours to run and people were moving in and out of the Hall, a steady buzz of discussion and purchasing going on the Main Room and, on occasion, the carrying of large and awkward packages to load into vans drawn up outside the main doors.

The Detective Inspector drew them into the judging room, which was still unavailable to the general public and had been cleared for use by the police. His exasperation was evident in his air of slight dishevelment; normally very neatly turned out with a precisely combed haircut, Jessica noted that today the Inspector's hair looked as if he had been running his hands through it, and his normally neatly pressed shirt was slightly untucked. And was that a stain on the lapel of his suit? Her speculations proved correct, as DI Gordon began to tell them about his morning, running one distracted hand over his head as he did so.

"You were absolute correct that the judging room door was locked, Miss Greer. However, it transpires that the same key will open both of the side rooms, and there were three keys in total. One was with your friend Miss Robertson, one in Mr Wilcott's possession, and the third was passed around amongst the stewards to give them access to the administration room during the judging." Jessica nodded, remembering a steward unlocking the door to the administration room when she had sat with Mrs Wilcott on Saturday.

DI Gordon continued: "In addition to that, the janitor has a master key which will open any interior door in the building, and do you know where that was? Hanging on a hook in the janitor's office under the stairs, which, by the way, was unlocked. No-one I've spoken to so far remembers anyone leaving or entering the preserves judging room after 9am, but the point is, anybody could have. And we had a constant stream of people between 9am and 11am, registering crafts, setting up display tables, sorting out the judging. Narrowing it down will be tricky.

"So, Constable Smith, determining access to the marmalade is proving to be harder than I'd hoped. Back to the drawing board I think, which in this instance means looking again for potential suspects, and then figuring out their movements. Did you have any luck in Dundee with finding out the identity of our anonymous newspaper correspondent?"

Murdo was cagey in his response. "No' really, Detective Inspector. We found plenty more letters, hard copies too, but nothing that said who it wis."

Jessica looked at him, surprised. "That's not quite true, DI Gordon. We did find one clue…"

She rummaged in her bag and pulled out a neat folder, within which the letter lay protected by a transparent plastic sleeve. Dr Ferguson had permitted it to be signed out of the Archives, although it was under Murdo's name as a representative of the police force. She held it in front of the Detective Inspector.

"We found this. It's quite old - and it looks like it was typed on an actual typewriter. But look here, in the corner. This is personalized stationery, it could tell us where McScunnered lives – or lived back then."

Murdo shook his head, interjecting now: "I telt Jessica there's no such place as Abbotsford Farm, no' these days. I've never heard of it. I'm sure there's maybe a way of finding it, but…"

The Detective Inspector looked at the letter, lips pursed. "Constable Smith is right, Miss Greer. I'm sure it could be very interesting to track down the building and find out who lived there, but from our perspective it's a dead-end. The trail is too cold, and with our limited resources, we would be far better to concentrate on the people that were currently in Mr Wilcott's life, and any information they might have to shed on who would have a grudge against him. It's highly likely that one of them will turn out to be McScunnered anyway. Thank you for bringing it to our attention and for visiting the archives, and I'm sorry that it wasn't more productive."

Jessica was disappointed. She had looked forward to continuing her investigation, and the presence of McScunnered meant that she had a legitimate reason to be assisting with the case in her capacity as junior reporter for *The Herald*. She wasn't sure what was driving her to help – a desire to solve the mystery?

Her innate sense of justice? Or was it that she felt instinctively that the finger would be pointed at Mrs Wilcott and she wanted to do everything in her power to prevent that from happening? Ever since overhearing her strained telephone conversation, Jessica had felt protective of the woman. This had only been compounded as she spent more time with her.

Jessica privately resolved to do everything she could to find McScunnered herself. DI Gordon and Murdo had turned slightly away from her and were engaged in conversation. Unnoticed, she slipped the plastic sleeve containing the old letter back into her bag.

After all, there was nothing stopping her doing some unrelated local history research, was there? Nothing at all.

9

A Wild Dash

Having taken her leave of Murdo and DI Gordon, Jessica went next door to the newspaper offices. She had gathered plenty of material for her piece on the Show that would appear that week, but hadn't yet pulled it all together into a coherent form – and after all, it wouldn't write itself. She found the office empty; Grant must be out reporting on something. She was grateful for the peace and quiet to get on and concentrate, but as always felt a pang of regret at Magnus' absence. He was rarely at the newspaper offices, and when he was there it was usually just to quickly upload his images, but she always enjoyed working alongside him whenever the occasion presented itself.

Despite this, Jessica worked steadily for the remainder of the afternoon. Grant didn't reappear at all, and by the time Jessica had finished her article she glanced at the clock and realised it was shop closing time, and that if she hurried down the hill she could catch Reenie and Willow at The Bloom Room and walk home through the park with them.

She emailed her article to Grant with a note saying that she would come to the office the next morning to go over any changes and finalise the copy for the deadline, and then she locked up the office and went down the stairs. The Show had closed half-an-hour earlier, and the car park opposite the Village Hall was full of people loading up their remaining crafts, stands and props. She spotted Ealisaid, busy in the middle of operations, and waved to her, gesturing that she was headed down the hill. Ealisaid shook her head and tapped at her watch – clearly indicating that her duties would keep her there for some time yet. Jessica marveled at her friend, currently single-handedly running a business and stepping up to do most of the Show Convenor duties since Desmond Wilcott's death. Ealisaid's sister Mairead had a certain amount of flexibility – she had recently decided to stay on in school for an optional 6th year, with a light timetable allowing her and sometimes a friend to work in the café – but even so, Jessica wondered how Ealisaid juggled everything. She had been the sole carer for her younger sister for the last decade, and on top of that plus the café, she had a small outside catering business and a long-distance relationship to throw into the mix as well. Solveig was an archaeologist, working on a summer-long dig somewhere up North, Jessica knew. The women rarely got a chance to spend any time together, but Jessica hoped to meet Solveig at Christmas time.

She knew that Ealisaid had not really had a choice about stepping up to carry through with the Show, but wondered if taking on the Convenor role as a permanent position was perhaps taking on too much. She resolved to have a chat with Ealisaid about it the next time they managed to catch up, and turning away, walked speedily down the hill towards the centre of Dalkinchie High Street. As she had suspected, Mairead was closing up in *Lissa's* and Reenie was doing the same, right across the street in The Bloom Room. Her timing couldn't have been better.

The Bloom Room bell pinged as she entered. She loved Reenie's shop, which was her aunt's pride and joy since setting up in business just a couple of months ago. She infinitely preferred it to her previous job as a florist for corporate events in the city, and even although she wasn't immune to the trials and tribulations of running her own business, life in Dalkinchie suited her perfectly. Jessica had initially only planned to stay for the summer, but had fallen in love with Dalkinchie herself. *Funny* she thought to herself *I'd be thinking about going back to school soon if I was at home.* Even as the thought crossed her mind, she realized how the word 'home' didn't seem like the correct one to use any more. Dalkinchie, Scotland: these were the places that the word 'home' was now conjuring up.

The shop wasn't large, but held a wonderful assortment of cut flowers and potted plants. The flowers were stored in a wrought iron rack at one side of the shop, and deep shelving held pots, vases and other accessories on the opposite wall. In the back left hand corner of the shop was a long, rich wooden counter, which was vintage and had been there when Reenie first rented the shop. She handled transactions there, and was able to do some floristry too, making up quick bouquets and hand-ties on the spot in front of customers. Dispensers behind the counter held ribbon and rolls of paper. A smaller unit sat in front of the counter held Reenie's selection of handmade potions, salves and bath salts. She grew the herbs she used herself, and Jessica knew that this was a side of the business

that she hoped to expand. Jessica inhaled deeply; the scent in
The Bloom Room was always beautiful and calming.

Willow greeted her enthusiastically. Jessica found two paws
planked just below her knee, and as she glanced down, the
puppy's expressive eyes gazed lovingly into her own. Her tail
was wagging so powerfully that she struggled to keep her bal-
ance. It was hard to reprimand her under these circumstances!
Jessica reached down to fondle Willow's silky ears, and the
puppy dropped to her feet and circled round her legs, sniffing
her jeans as she always did when Jessica had spent any time in
the newspaper offices. She must be picking up Skye's scent.

"Just in time Jessica, I'm cashing up!" Reenie called from the
back shop, and a few moments later she emerged, having locked
the cash and banking away in a small, stout safe she used for
that purpose. Dalkinchie didn't have a bank branch, instead
relying on a mobile service that visited the village twice a week,
and Drummond on one further occasion.

With the locking up accomplished, the two women made their
way back home to the cottage on their accustomed path through
the park. Reenie had picked Jessica up from the bus stop earlier,
and had therefore heard all about the trip to Dundee, but since
then had apparently had a visitor in the form of Grant who had
popped in to the shop to have a quick coffee on the way to a
reporting job.

"Oh, yes?" Jessica's ears pricked up. She had spotted the
chemistry between her aunt and Grant the first time that
she had met him. Reenie had been single for a long time
after losing her husband tragically early – Jessica had never
known her Uncle Alistair, although he was present in the
many photographs that Reenie displayed around her home.
Since arriving in Dalkinchie, Reenie and Grant had become

undeniably closer, going for occasional drinks together and on one occasion, dinner – but Grant's caring responsibilities prevented him from having much of a social life, and for her part Reenie seemed content to work on settling in to Dalkinchie and establishing her business, with not much time or energy left over for romance. This seemed to suit them both, but frustrated Jessica, who loved her aunt dearly and was becoming very fond of her boss, a genuine and kind man.

"Nothing like that Jessica! He just found himself nearby and in need of a wee caffeine boost, I think. You are a terrible girl! I wouldn't have thought you'd be interested – the age of the pair of us. We're ancient!"

"Hardly! Everyone deserves happiness, Reenie. You are so good for each other."

"Well, we are good friends, I'll give you that. Don't be in too much of a rush though. I certainly enjoy the time I spend with Grant, but he's got a lot on his plate and so do I. This little one, for starters. Although she's being a very good girl today!"

Willow was bouncy, but walking quite nicely along the path. At least, she had been walking quite nicely up until this point, but as Reenie uttered her words the pup spotted a flash of movement in the distance and was off, pulling her leash from Reenie's grip and dashing away down the path – in the wrong direction from the cottage.

"I spoke too soon," Reenie groaned, just as Jessica said, "you jinxed it!" and gave chase after the small white-and-tan puppy.

For a young puppy, Willow was really fast. She dived down the path, shadowed overhead by the thick green foliage of high beech trees. Her leash trailed uselessly behind her as she found her legs and sped like an arrow away from Jessica. Reenie had unearthed some treats from her jacket pocket and was calling

"Wil-low! Wil-low!", using the high-pitched tone they had been advised by the dog trainer to employ in situations such as these. It didn't work. The puppy was too young to have learned a good recall, and while Jessica fancied that Willow had first spotted a squirrel and had run after it, she was now running for the sheer, glorious freedom of unchecked speed and motion. At least Jessica was managing to keep her in sight, and at least Willow was keeping to the path.

After many weeks of largely sunny weather the dirt path was packed down and dry, but underneath these trees it was always in deep shade. The surface was uneven, tree roots running underneath it here and there, and Jessica had to watch where she was placing her feet. Not Willow. She practically flew over the knobbly surface and seemed, if anything, to be picking up speed as she went. Jessica had followed this particular path only once before. It took you deep into the wilder parts of the park, the open grassy areas and children's play equipments left behind and replaced with steep banks down to the Burn. A profusion of wildflowers and weeds covered the banks at the sides of the path. Despite the untouched nature of this part of the park, there were still signs of civilisation here and there. An occasional bench along the route. Garbage bins. Steps leading down from the main path to a small decked area below, adjacent to the Burn. Jessica even noticed some small carved figures, peeking from the trees. She must ask Reenie about them some time. She believed that this path eventually joined up with another road in Dalkinchie, and wanted to catch Willow before she could make it that far.

All of a sudden, Willow seemed to tire and came to a stop. She stood, panting, as Jessica slowed down herself and walked carefully up to her, not wanting to startle the puppy into bolting again. It seemed that this was the last thing on the dog's mind, however, as she turned to Jessica and obediently came to her, the leash slithering over the path in her wake. Jessica reached down and picked it up, wrapping it around her wrist for good measure, and then, dog secured, she bent over and brushed Willow down. The pup had picked up some grass, wood chippings and leaves on her flight and they were sticking to her fur. Willow stood patiently for this, even nuzzling Jessica's leg.

Jessica was about to turn and leave to find Reenie again when she caught sight of someone in the distance, further along the path. Ahead of Jessica and Willow it followed a slight incline upwards and then curved left and went down again. There was thick foliage between them, meaning that from where Jessica stood she could just see a green coat and the back of someone's head – a distinctive cloud of apricot-coloured hair. Jessica, still unsure if she knew the person, adjusted her position to get a clearer view which confirmed that it was indeed, Margaret Mustard. But what was she doing?

Margaret was behaving most unlike her usual self. Never one for dodging the spotlight, she stood hunched and crouched, as if to make herself appear smaller, and head bowed, she was taking quick, furtive glances around. She was looking in the wrong direction to spot Jessica however, and as the latter watched, Margaret took out a bundle from under her coat. It was wrapped in a plastic bag from a grocery store and as Jessica watched, she realised what Margaret was doing. There was a trash can where she stood, the square, black type with a cover and an opening at the top of each face. Margaret Mustard manoeuvred her package through one of the openings and in to the trash, and, Jessica still watching, she reached right inside, clearly lowering the bundle as far as she could. It finally landed inside with a heavy thud. Margaret withdrew her arm, took another surreptitious look around, and then, still not spotting Jessica, she left, moving along the path in the opposite direction. The whole time Willow hadn't made a sound, clearly shattered from her escape.

Jessica stood, deep in thought. What could Margaret Mustard want to get rid of so badly that she had to do so in secret in the middle of the dark paths of the park?

* * *

Jessica had to leave the question unanswered. Reenie had caught up with them, and Willow had pulled towards her, then behaved with contrition, whimpering and rubbing herself against Reenie's legs. After making sure the little dog had had a drink, Reenie for her part was concerned about Willow's developing muscles – the advice was short walks on lead only for the first few months, and no-one had said anything about a mad dash across a country park.

The two women had ended up taking it in turns to carry the puppy home, much as they had done in the first few weeks after bringing her home, before she had completed her vaccination schedule. She didn't seem to be any the worse for her escapade, wolfing down her dinner and sleeping soundly for most of the night, apart from her usual training trip to the garden.

There had been no time to think about it the next morning either, as Reenie and Jessica both breakfasted and hurried to their workplaces. *The Drummond and Dalkinchie Herald* was printed on a Wednesday, so Tuesdays were quite often a rush of finalising last minute copy. Jessica went straight to the newspaper offices to check that Grant was happy with the article she had sent him the evening before, and to find out if there was anything else he required her to do.

"It's wonderful, Jessica – clear, respectful, and you have all the information about this year's Show that anyone could possibly need. You've chosen excellent retrospective pieces to showcase as well. Well done. You really have a flair for archival research – it would be great if you could do more pieces along these lines in the future."

Grant's feedback was always well thought out and genuinely useful. Jessica had begun to feel as if she knew what she was doing, gathering information, shaping it into a coherent piece for the local audience, and writing it up quickly. If she was honest with herself, her choice of journalism as a career had been more to do with it seeming like the next logical step after her English Lit major, and the fact that she could study it at the same grad school as her now ex-boyfriend, Mike. It had been a terrible basis on which to make decisions, she now realized, and although his decision to dump her just before graduation had broken her heart at the time, she was beginning to think that he might have done her an enormous favor. Mike was the reason that she was in Scotland at all, having canceled her plans to spend the summer working as camp counselors together before grad school. She vastly preferred her current situation and knew that if she were to decide to pick up her deferred journalism place at grad school the following year, it would be coming from a place of genuine interest and a passion for studying the subject.

"Do you need me for anything this morning, Grant?"

"Not right now, Jessica. Your four-page spread has cut down on the amount of work I have to do, so thank you for that. If you give me a call later, there's a small reporting job that I might need you and Magnus to cover, but right now please take a break."

Jessica nodded. This was the usual pattern on a Tuesday. She hadn't yet learned any design or layout skills, and both freelancer desks in the outer office were occupied today – one by Magnus, who was finalizing his photo edits, and the other by Marian Sheddon, a woman who came in once a week on deadline day to pull together all the diary entries submitted by locals and community groups in both Drummond and Dalkinchie. In it were items like fundraising efforts, local events, and notices for long-running groups. Classes and promotional services were permitted as well, although no direct advertising – for that people had to pay. She also compiled the 'News from our Schools' section and the Births, Marriages and Deaths notices. She was a friendly woman and had smiled at Jessica as she came in, but had no time for small-talk – she did all her work in one day to ensure that it was as up-to-date as possible. Grant had told Jessica that she had been there for a couple of decades, long predating his time as editor of *The Herald* and had been an enormous help to him when he first started, but that she had no interest in taking on any more work beyond her one day per week.

Happy to be getting a break, Jessica headed down the hill with the intention of checking whether Reenie needed any help in The Bloom Room, and, if not, treating herself to brunch at *Lissa's*. If Ealisaid wasn't too busy, she might be able to catch up with her as well. Her plans changed, however, when she bumped into Patricia Wilcott outside the coffee shop.

"Jessica, how lovely to see you. Are you in a hurry? I was just going to go in for a cup of tea. You would be more than welcome to join me – my treat." Patricia looked well, considering, her eyes bright and her voice animated. She was pale, but then she was the type of woman that Jessica suspected would always be pale, her skin almost translucent in places. The purplish shadows under her eyes indicated that she perhaps wasn't getting enough sleep, but apart from that she seemed fine.

Jessica glanced over at The Bloom Room. Reenie was within, attending to one customer while another browsed the vases of flowers; she didn't seem swamped. Jessica made up her mind.

"Thanks Patricia, I would love to have some tea with you. It doesn't have to be your treat though, I was thinking of having brunch myself anyway. I was in a hurry this morning and only grabbed a banana for breakfast."

Patricia's smile widened. "Wonderful. I insist on paying, however. I might join you in a snack. I'm partial to Ealisaid's hot rolls."

They made their way into the café, and as ever, Jessica was struck by the cozy ambience and friendly feel. Over the last few months she had realized just how important *Lissa's* was as the centre of the community, serving as a hub for information, sustenance and promoting local business and services. Ealisaid herself was dealing with her usual line of morning customers, but still managed to glance up and wave at Jessica and Patricia as they came in. The café was filling up but Jessica found a table for two, nestled in one of the back corners. While Patricia went up to order the food and drinks, she sat and fiddled with a tiny vase which held a sprig of heather. She didn't see anyone she recognised in the café apart from Ealisaid herself.

Patricia returned, carrying two mugs, and behind her was a teenager that Jessica didn't recognise, carrying a tray with a large white porcelain teapot, and milk jug and sugar bowl. There was also a wooden spoon with a number painted on the bowl, which the young waiter slotted into the holder on the table, created for that very purpose. This was how Ealisaid managed her food orders, saving the need to shout them out over the hubbub of a busy café.

"How are you, Patricia?"

"To be honest with you, I'm not sure Jessica. Everywhere I look there seems to be another job to do, something else to sort out, another form to fill in. I'm keeping going purely on adrenaline I think – I don't even remember if I ate breakfast this morning, which is why this is such a good idea. I am in Dalkinchie this morning to pick up the car. It has been parked outside the Village Hall since Saturday, and it only just occurred to me that I have a spare car key and I could fetch it any time I liked! That's an example of how scattered I have been." Patricia shook her head, as if in despair at herself, and moved to pour tea in first Jessica's, then her own mug.

"I'm sure that is totally normal. It would be stranger if you just carried on as if nothing had happened." Jessica wondered if this was perhaps the wrong thing to say – was there any normal in this situation? She had heard of people reacting to grief in all sorts of ways, and this was more than grief – there was the ongoing police investigation, too.

Patricia smiled. "You are right, of course. You really do remind me of my daughter, Helen. The same knack for knowing what to say."

Jessica realized, not for the first time, that she should trust her instincts more and stop second-guessing herself. She was about to answer when the same young waiter arrived, bringing their rolls. She had gone for a bacon roll with tattie scone, a Scottish speciality – a flat, triangular item that was more like a pancake than a scone, and made of a combination of flour and mashed potato. They were a very popular breakfast food here. Patricia was also having a typical Scottish morning roll, but she had clearly requested the 'well-fired' type as her bread roll was darker on top. Hers contained a fried egg. Jessica loved the morning rolls, with a dry (but not too chewy) exterior, and a soft (but not too doughy) interior, it was no wonder that most of the other people in *Lissa's* were also tucking into one. Ealisaid bought them in bulk from the bakery next door to her café, along with the potato scones and sliced loaves for her sandwiches. She baked all the cakes and scones herself.

She added some HP brown sauce to hers and then tucked in. Patricia, meanwhile, took a dainty bite. Jessica marveled at the woman's ability to eat a fried egg roll so tidily. "Mmm, delicious. Thank you, Jessica, for reminding me to eat! With my usual routines disrupted and no-one in the house to cook for, I could easily forget."

"You're welcome. That's not something I ever have a problem remembering! Will you have someone to cook for soon – I mean, is your daughter traveling home to spend some time here?"

Patricia sighed. She took a sip of tea before replying. "I wish she was Jessica, but it's complicated. I've actually had Donald over this morning trying to help me figure it out. Helen originally moved to Australia with her husband – his job took him there. They have a child, my little granddaughter, Evie." Patricia paused, her eyes lighting up, clearly delighted by the thought of the child. "However, in recent months, Helen and her husband's relationship has…broken down, and in fact they are separated. Helen moved out, taking the child, very recently. However, they are not divorced."

"Helen and Mark married here," she continued, "but moved

to Australia before having Evie, and she is actually an Australian citizen. She doesn't have a passport of any sort yet. We have always traveled to visit her. Helen now wants to return to the U.K. Mark, understandably, doesn't want her to do that because he wouldn't be able to see his daughter as much. He is making it very difficult for Helen to apply for a passport for their daughter, and is threatening her with lawyers if she attempts to bring Evie here, even if just for a visit. He doesn't trust her. For her part, Helen doesn't want to come home without Evie. She is worried about what Mark might be able to achieve with regards to custody in her absence. It really is a mess, and on top of all that Helen has been a stay-at-home mum since Evie was born, meaning that she has no money or resources to get lawyers of her own over there. I have been supporting her as best I can, but..."

Patricia tailed off, looking towards the café window for a moment. Her eyes had misted over, and she seemed lost in reflection for a moment or two. Then she resumed: "It's difficult, from such a distance away."

Jessica really didn't know how to respond this time. What could she possibly offer? It seemed like such a hopelessly fraught issue, and a specialist one at that, probably requiring a family lawyer. Her own mom was a lawyer, but not one that handled divorces or custody issues – and she practised in the States. Australia would undoubtedly be different. She waited for Patricia to regain her thoughts, topping up both of their mugs with hot tea from the pot. The sympathy she already felt for Patricia had increased tenfold. How was the woman coping?

Patricia came to, and nodded her thanks. "I'm sorry to have bombarded you with all of that, Jessica. It's not your concern.

It's just weighing heavily on my mind at the moment, that's all, and with Desmond's death, it has really made it more urgent that we sort something out. Let's change the subject. What have you been up to?"

"Actually, I was hoping to talk to you about that, if you don't mind. The police were interested in the feud your husband had with the letter-writer in the newspaper, and I ended up going to Dundee yesterday to try and verify their identity. Have they asked you about it?"

"About McScunnered? Not specifically, no. They have asked about anyone he had a run-in with. In all honesty, Jessica, it's a long list. He put people's backs up, and his actions sometimes had very unfortunate consequences as well. If I was to rank his feuds, I wouldn't put McScunnered very high at all. If anything, I got the impression that the two of them almost enjoyed the letter-writing, back and forth."

"Did your husband...Mr Wilcott ever suspect who it might have been?"

"He speculated, definitely, but never found out for sure as far as I am aware. I didn't pay too much attention to be honest. It was just another of his obsessions, typing away at that computer of his. I know that he thought it was probably somebody he had worked with, or that knew somebody else at the bank well. Some details were too specific to be common knowledge, he said. Have you heard about what happened at the bank?"

"Yes...at least, I have heard some of it. I know that something happened, and some people lost their jobs."

"That's part of it. In truth, it was part of a much bigger problem. This was one occasion where Desmond really was not at fault. The whole bank went under, and had to be bailed out by the British government – do you know anything about this? I'm not sure whether it would have made the news in the U.S.A., but it was a big deal here at the time. It was connected to the big global financial crisis, of course. Desmond really had nothing to do with it at all. He unfortunately was in charge of restructuring the departments at the offices here, and had to make a number of people redundant. He was not unaffected – none of the management team received a bonus that year, and in fact he retired on a lesser package than he would have been due to receive if circumstances had been different. There's no point telling anyone that around here though, and I'm certainly not saying he was badly off – it was still an extremely comfortable retirement package, and I quite understand the resentment that built up. It did become very nasty at times."

"Why, what happened?" Jessica encouraged Patricia to continue.

"People started to make scenes at the various committees that Desmond was a member of. Drummond and Dalkinchie are actually relatively small communities, and it seemed that everyone knew someone who had been affected by the re-dundancies, and felt like airing their grievances at committee meetings. Desmond would become incredibly frustrated that people were bringing their personal matters into committee business and on one particularly memorable occasion, someone resigned from the committee and walked out, after calling him something…a pernickety old goat, that was it! He thought it *highly* inappropriate!"

"Who was that? Was it – "

"It was Margaret Mustard. One of the worst parts was that I believe she had planned the confrontation in advance and had persuaded her cronies to walk out with her – but when push came to shove, everybody shrank back in their seats and didn't follow her out. So she also fell out with some of her friends, and then she held *that* against Desmond as well, of course."

Margaret Mustard. Again. Could Margaret Mustard be McScunnered? One and the same? She fit the criteria of being close to someone who worked in the bank, and although Desmond Wilcott had believed McScunnered to be a man, Jessica had found nothing that definitively stated this. In addition, although Jessica knew that Margaret Mustard lived in Dalkinchie and not in Drummond, she certainly considered Castle Drummond her second home and might use that address for her alternative persona. Suddenly, she felt the need to speak to Murdo and see if she could get any information from him on where the police suspicions lay.

Patricia was still speaking. "Anyway, Desmond never bothered about whether people liked him or not. He just wanted to be in charge, and get things done. He was not unlike our son-in-law Mark, in that regard. The two of them clashed horribly on our visits over there, especially as we tended to stay for a number of weeks to make it worth the journey. We were due to go out together again, actually, next week."

Jessica was confused. This surely could not be the case; it directly contradicted the conversation she had overheard Patricia having on her cell phone on Saturday morning. On that call, she had been very clear that she would be traveling to Australia alone. Why would Patricia lie to her about it? But before she had a chance to ask, she received a text message from Grant. She had been half-expecting one, as he had said there might be a story to report on later, but what she read when she opened it made her sit up straighter in her seat, so focused that the rest of the sound of the café was blocked out:

"Jessica. Would you be able to come to the office ASAP? We have been processing the letters to the editor and there's one final one here from McScunnered. It would be good to have your opinion. Grant."

10

Shortbread at the Castle

"Hello, Jessica. Thank you for coming back in. I did think it would be best if you could take a look at this. Two heads are better than one!"

Jessica moved into Grant's inner office where she was greeted by his beautiful black labrador, Skye. Always a gentle dog, Jessica had cause to appreciate her dignity even more lately as a comparison to the wild bundle of fluff and teeth she had to deal with at home. Skye moved slowly and elegantly, rising from her soft tartan bed that lay under the window, and stretching deeply before padding unhurriedly over to Jessica and lifting her muzzle up for a scratch behind her ears.

"Hello again, Skye," Jessica said softly and Skye stood for a few moments more, then turned and moved at the same pace back to her bed where she curled up and rested her chin on the edge, steadily observing Jessica as she sat down. Jessica found the dog's presence hugely comforting, and knew that she had been spoiled for future jobs. It would probably not be reasonable to make an office dog a condition of working somewhere, although she really felt that they should be mandatory in every workplace.

She turned to Grant.

"Another letter from McScunnered. Did it arrive in the mail? What does it say?"

"Yes, it was just in the bundle of post with some others. That's how they have always arrived, and I don't think it's significant. I get emails, but still plenty of written letters too, some of them hand-delivered. Not McScunnered though, nor Desmond Wilcott for that matter. They always used good old Royal Mail, and usually a first class stamp. As for what it says, you had probably best take a look yourself."

He handed Jessica a long rectangular brown envelope. The post-mark betrayed nothing other than it had been posted locally the day before, which was entirely as she would have expected. She flipped the envelope open and drew out the letter within. Folded into thirds, it was exactly like most of the hard copy letters she had seen at the Dundee City Archives. Word-processed on white printer paper, no personalization. The heading contained only a date. McScunnered did not like to share his/her address.

"Dear Sir,

I refer to the unfortunate demise of Mr Desmond Wilcott, and wish to extend my condolences to his family and friends for their loss. I could not say that I considered him a friend, but I have certainly enjoyed the cut and thrust of debate in these very pages over the years. He and I differed on many things, but he was a force to be reckoned with and I acknowledge that he achieved a lot for the community, even if he often went about it in entirely reprehensible ways.

Had I known it was to be his final hour, I would have spent

longer talking to him on the morning of his exit. As it is, I wish this to be my last goodbye to the man who, more than any other, kept my wit sharp and my pen quick over the last decade and a half.

Yours faithfully,

McScunnered of Drummond."

Jessica found herself unexpectedly moved. She read over it again.

"It's quite touching in a way, isn't it?" Grant had obviously noticed her reaction.

"It's the bit about 'the man who kept my wits sharp', it just gets to me. I suppose McScunnered has suffered a loss as well."

"Yes. The loss of an adversary shouldn't be underestimated, and it doesn't seem as if McScunnered has done so. However, you will have noticed the reason I asked you to take a look at it?" Grant looked questioningly at Jessica.

"Yes. So Desmond Wilcott actually spoke to McScunnered on Saturday morning? I suppose that means McScunnered was at the Show – although, it could have been earlier that morning, before the Show. I suppose I could ask Patricia if they talked to anyone before arriving. If it *was* at the Show, then I suppose there are lots of people it could still be. It does narrow it down a little, although probably not enough to be worth bothering DI Gordon. He's already tearing his hair out at the number of potential suspects who could have had access to the marmalade. Actually, I had a thought, Grant – do you think that Margaret Mustard could be McScunnered? She fits the criteria in a lot of ways…"

"No." Grant's reply was decisive. Jessica looked at him in surprise.

"I mean, I really don't think so. Sorry to be so adamant. You are right to consider it and it is, of course, technically possible. I just cannot see it, however. Margaret writes a lot – snippets for the Diary section, the occasional letter herself, in the Parish newsletter – and I therefore know her writing style well. It couldn't be more different from McScunnered, and I also just can't see her having the ability to invent an alter ego with their own voice, and stick to it for so long. Margaret is many things, but she's not duplicitous. No. I'm ninety-nine percent certain that we are dealing with someone else. I have been meaning to ask you actually, can I have a look at the letter that you found at the archives? I'm assuming you still have it, or did DI Gordon hold on to it?"

"I still have it. He didn't believe it was really evidence, so I planned on keeping it here actually; I should have filed it with our records until we could return it to the archives."

She drew the letter from her bag, still in its protective plastic sleeve. Grant looked it over carefully. "This one is surely before my time. It looks like it has been typed on a typewriter. I see what you mean about the farmhouse, it must be very tempting to see if you can track that down. It doesn't exist any more?"

Jessica was glad that someone understood her compulsion to follow this lead.

"No, Murdo said there was no such farm now. I think the shape of the house is quite distinctive though, and I can't see why it would have been demolished – surely it probably still stands, even if not on a farm and not called Abbotsford any longer?"

"I should think that is entirely accurate, yes. I presume that that farm land was probably sold off for development, and the farmhouse itself remains a private dwelling, probably now close to some newer houses. That's happened on a few sites around here. Look."

Grant moved over to one of his large wooden bookcases. Lying along the top of it he kept a few maps, long and rolled within sturdy cardboard outer tubes. He drew one down and checked the description printed on one end, returned it and drew down another. This he opened and spread across his large wooden desk, which he always kept clear and free of clutter. Jessica assisted by placing paperweights at two of the four corners while Grant held down the other two.

"This is a map of Dalkinchie and Drummond around fifty years ago. You can see here that there are many more green spaces than there are now – it's still very green of course, but from time to time a farmer will decide to sell his land for development instead of continuing to work the land, if he didn't have anyone to pass it on to. It has historically been a 'he', although we are seeing more women take on farming these days and being very enterprising – a wonderful thing, in my opinion. Individual farm names are not marked here, but it might give you a starting point."

"A starting point? I don't know, Grant, I'm not sure now whether I should pursue it any further and I would have to find transport to Drummond."

"Well, you see, that's the thing. I have a small job for you this afternoon. Very easy – just nip along to Drummond Primary School to attend the Primary One welcoming presentation, and write it up for next week's paper. Magnus will drive you, as he will be taking new class photos anyway. While you are there, I don't see that it would do any harm to have a quick look round the areas and see if you can spot anything that resembles the house here. Magnus will also be helpful in that regard as he's sure to know what used to be farmland as well. What do you say?"

Jessica couldn't prevent a wide smile from taking over her face. A fun, easy job, an afternoon with Magnus and an opportunity to follow up on a fascinating clue?

"I say, you're the boss, Boss!"

* * *

Magnus turned the steering wheel smoothly to the left, and they drove up a leafy residential street in Drummond. It had looked from the map that this area had been farmland at approximately the right time, and while the houses here were newer, they definitely were not brand new – a couple of decades old, at least. Jessica had tried to sketch the little farmhouse a bit larger, capturing the distinctive outline of the house which had a large gable end and, it looked like, a smaller outbuilding that peeked out the side. There was also a sketch of a tall spiny tree beside it – possibly the tree would still be there?

There was, however, no shortage of trees, and none of the older stone houses Magnus and Jessica drove past looked enough like the one in her sketch to warrant further investigation. Jessica admitted temporary defeat. It was time to head to the primary school for their Primary One welcoming ceremony.

The tiny children were delightful in their impossibly cute school uniforms. Jessica hadn't known that you could get school shirts, formal trousers and blazers that small, but the children certainly looked adorable and were very enthusiastic. They had learned a song in their first day at school and belted it out to the gathered parents.

The MacNaughton was also present, poised to hand out a gym bag to each child in a short presentation after the ceremony. Magnus captured this, and was also ready to group the children together in their classes with their individual teachers and take photos for the paper – something, he had explained to Jessica, that happened every year. It also took place in the same spot every time, beside a large shady tree in the school grounds.

Jessica thoroughly enjoyed the ceremony, and it wouldn't be hard at all to write up. She made sure she knew the name of the song, and of the teachers. After that, she just watched as the children lined up for their photos – a task which proved to be not unlike herding cats, but the atmosphere was relaxed and good-natured. The event had been timed for the last hour of school so that parents could take the children home afterwards. The bell rang, signalling the end of the school day, and Jessica, Magnus and the MacNaughton signed out at the main office and headed to the car park together.

"Here – I'd promised your dad something, Magnus, a jar of that salve that we'd thought might work for the coo wi' the sore leg? Would you have the time just noo to pop up for it? Might as well, get it to him that bit quicker if you were no' in a hurry."

Magnus looked at Jessica, who nodded – she certainly didn't have anywhere urgent to be, and the thought of visiting Castle Drummond was thrilling. She had seen photos and read up a little on its history, but as yet had not had the occasion to visit. She was more than happy to 'pop up'!

"Aye, I'll take ye up on that, Gillespie. Thanks very much. My dad will be awfy grateful, he's been concerned about Meg, on and off. It's no' really bad and she's fine in herself, milking is fine, so he's no' called the vet, but there's definitely a wee twinge here and there, as if she's just moved it funny."

132

"This stuff works wonders. Coos, sheep, pigs – it's just a muscle rub, but I've half a jar left, and there's no point your dad buying some when he can try it, an' see if it works. Just follow me up then, and I'll see you there."

Castle Drummond sat slightly above the village, its vantage point betraying its history as a defensive keep. The straight-sided rectangular stone building was in fact the section of the castle that was most visible from the village below, and today, as ever, it boasted a single Saltire flag, the white cross on the blue background fluttering in the afternoon's stiff breeze. The castle dated from the fifteenth century, but an extension added some 250 years later formed the main living residence for the MacNaughton. Jessica knew that he held occasional Clan Gatherings there, and wondered what it must be like to see it full of people in full kilted regalia.

They followed the MacNaughton's rattly Land Rover up the narrow, winding road and then turned left through large, impos-ing gates – which, Magnus informed Jessica, were permanently propped open. The MacNaughton, as the Laird of Drummond, managed a lot of the neighbouring estate, and tenant farmers were always popping in and out – and other people too. He was famously friendly. The Smiths' own farm Balnaguise was not part of the Drummond estate, but Magnus had spent plenty of time there anyway. Farmers stick together.

After driving through the gate, Magnus drew to a halt in front of the castle. Jessica looked around with undisguised interest. The section to the right was the original keep, a blocky rectangular building of ancient weathered stones and narrow slits of windows. She remembered from previous castle tours that the word for the gaps in the walls was 'crenels' but she couldn't remember the other words. It was topped with proper battlements, and Jessica thrilled at the thought of what must have taken place there. Fighting off the English, and occasionally other Scots as well, she thought.

The rest of Drummond castle was more rambling, a higgledy piggledy mish mash of buildings joined on to the original. She spotted a turret in one corner and stout chimneys adorning the centre of the roof. The windows here were larger, built to let light in rather than to shoot arrows from. Above two of them thistle and ivy were carved into arched stone lintels which also proclaimed '*I HOIP IN GOD*'. The views from this vantage point over Drummond were already breathtaking, sweeping over the land to the purplish hills beyond, and Jessica realized that they must be exceptional from the high points of the castle.

"Come away in!" The MacNaughton had pulled his car up too, on the rough gravel just adjacent to a green lawn that circled the property. His thick boots crunched over the path as he led them around the side of the building and held a heavy wooden door open for them.

It led straight into a large kitchen. Jessica had an impression of space, a huge stone flagged floor, wooden beams running across the ceiling and an absolutely enormous range stove set in an alcove at the back of the room. A series of pulleys ran down the length of the kitchen ceiling, used variously as pot racks and drying racks for clothes. Bundles of herbs were hanging there too, giving a woody, sweet smell to the whole room. A large, scrubbed wooden table, which would have completely filled any kitchen Jessica had ever set foot in before, took up about a third of the floor space. Everything was cluttered, but immaculately clean, the table clear and free of crumbs, the old slate floor swept.

"Tea?"

Even in this enormous room the MacNaughton looked larger than life, his expansive personality, big beard and booming voice filling the kitchen. Both Magnus and Jessica accepted his offer and Gillespie McNaughton strode down to the stove where a large metal kettle sat, picked it up with one hand and casually filled it from the taps above a deep, square porcelain sink beneath the window – a Belfast sink, Jessica thought they were called. He lifted one of the round metal plates and placed the kettle on top of the stove where it immediately began to stir. Jessica realised that the stove must be permanently hot.

"Margaret's been in today, but she's always away by this time. She's done a grand job as usual, and if I'm no' mistaken, will have left us a wee something in the pantry." There was a door on either side of the stove alcove; the MacNaughton disappeared through one of them and reappeared within seconds, triumphantly bearing a platter covered in a snowy white cloth with blue stitched edges. As he did so, the kettle on top of the stove began to sing.

"We're in luck! Petticoat tails. Who would like a piece?"

"Oh aye, that would be just the thing." Magnus replied, saying as an aside to Jessica, "Margaret's shortbread is some of the finest you'll ever taste."

He wasn't wrong. Jessica accepted a piece of the crumbly, triangular baked delicacy along with the enormous mug of steaming hot tea that was soon pressed into her hand. Both were delicious, the shortbread buttery, slightly gritty, perfectly sweet and almost melting in her mouth. The tea stopped just short of too strong, and Jessica found it incredibly reviving. Sitting here at the kitchen table, in a Laird's kitchen, having just been made a cup of tea by him – she could almost have been dreaming. She hadn't realised how tired she was, but her energy returned as she ate and drank. Magnus and the MacNaughton tucked in too, all three in a companionable silence.

Magnus was the first to speak again. "Gillespie – have you ever heard tell of Abbotsford Farm? Long gone noo – but we've been trying to find where it was. A wee history project."

The MacNaughton looked thoughtful. "Abbotsford...Abbotsford...the name sounds familiar, but I cannae mind right noo. Why don't you both come through to the study and I'll see what I can find."

Jessica and Magnus both followed as the MacNaughton led the way through the other side door at the far end of the kitchen. The study was exactly as Jessica would have pictured. Ornate, carved, dark wood furniture, including a desk inlaid with dark green leather, and massive bookcases filled with bound volumes. She ached to have a look through them. A rich burgundy carpet was underfoot, patterned with small gold diamonds. In one corner of the room, a wooden bust sat on a tall unit. Every available surface was covered with sheaves of papers and folders, and the desk also held open notebooks containing pencilled scribbles.

The MacNaughton scratched his head. "I apologise for the mess. My solicitor's been up a few times and we've been trying to get some of the papers in order. We are still working on it. Anyway, maybe these would be what you'd need – land registers, going back a couple o' hundred years." He knelt down at the base of one of the bookcases and ran a finger along the large volumes stored there. There must have been at least thirty of them. "Either of you would be welcome to take a look if that would help?"

Jessica looked gratefully at him, and secretly there was nothing she would like more than poring over old ledgers in the Castle Drummond study, but she knew it would turn into a lengthy task and that Magnus would have evening duties at the farm. "That would be great, thanks! If we don't find it I will definitely take you up on that. I think we need to get back to Dalkinchie now, though – get that salve to your dad, Magnus."

"We do indeed, but thanks Gillespie. I'd be interested in taking a look. I bet Balnaguise features in those old registers."

"Oh, more than once, Magnus, more than once. Any time, just let me know."

The MacNaughton escorted them back through to the kitchen where Jessica and Magnus thanked him again and took their leave, Jessica conscious that Magnus had duties on the farm. She asked him to drop her in Dalkinchie High Street, where she planned to assist Reenie with closing up The Bloom Room before heading home for the evening.

Magnus did so, waving as he left, leaving Jessica smiling as she watched the car drive off. Turning, she almost bumped into Margaret Mustard who was about to head into *Lissa's*. Her next words changed Jessica's plans once again.

"Oh Jessica – it's yourself! Have you heard? It's Patricia Wilcott. She's been arrested!"

11

Patricia and the Poison

Jessica followed Margaret into *Lissa's* where everyone was abuzz with this new information. Her head was spinning. How could this be? She had only been speaking to Patricia that morning – what could possibly have happened in the interim that had led to her arrest?

Margaret joined a large group of women who had pushed two tables together near the front of the café. One of them vacated her seat in order to usher Margaret into it, and another went looking for a spare chair to squeeze around the table to accommodate her. They were all agog.

Jessica couldn't help but overhear them as they began to speak, and the general consensus seemed to be that while the Wilcotts had always seemed like a solid couple and Patricia Wilcott a pleasant enough woman, you just couldn't know people at all, and there was no smoke without fire. But anyway they had always suspected that there was something 'off' about her, after all why would her daughter move to the other side of the world – maybe it was to get away from her? Who was to say what went on behind closed doors. And poison, well, that was just like her really, she could be quite sneaky – in fact, quite an unpleasant woman all told.

"Well, I don't want to say I told you so, but…" Miss Janet Simpson trailed off and pursed her lips together primly. Had she said any such thing, Jessica wondered, or was she just taking the credit now?

"It's no surprise to me. Mind that time I told you that Patricia Wilcott ignored me in McEwen's greengrocers? Just flat out ignored me, and rushed off without saying a word." The woman who had spoken these words shook her head before taking a sip of tea.

Grateful that none of these people were in charge of determining Patricia Wilcott's guilt or otherwise, Jessica turned towards the counter to check if Ealisaid was free. It was late in the afternoon, past both the lunchtime rush and the afternoon tea crowd, and normally at this time *Lissa's* would be quieter. Although some customers were drinking hot drinks, Jessica couldn't see many plates on tables and there was no-one ordering anything. Margaret had come in and sat down without so much as a glance at the menu.

Jessica's own reaction surprised her. Somehow, without knowing exactly when or how, she had become convinced of Patricia Wilcott's innocence. She was aware that she personally liked the woman, becoming more fond of her and feeling more empathy every time they spoke. Perhaps she was allowing this to cloud her judgement? If you examined the evidence…she thought to herself for a minute. What evidence was there really? Had the police found something else new?

Her question was soon answered. Ealisaid was available behind the counter, not serving anyone and happy to chat.

"Don't you mind everyone coming in and using your place

as a...gossip hub?" Jessica was indignant now on her friend's behalf, having done a rough count of the number of drinks on tables and knowing that this was cutting into Ealisaid's clearing up time.

"No' really. I set this place up to be a centre of the community, so I can hardly blame them for using it that way. They more than make up for it on most days – despite the fact that almost every one of them here is excellent at baking, they are forever in here ordering mine. They donate all their own cakes to fundraising sales and coffee mornings. It's just the way it works around here."

Jessica nodded, appreciating her friend's shrewd business sense once again. Then she confided in her. "Ealisaid, I'm really shocked! Patricia Wilcott has been arrested? I was only just here chatting to her this morning! What could have happened?"

"Aye, according to the locals she has been arrested. I wouldnae take it as confirmed quite yet. I dinnae know what happened; she left just after you this morning and I've not seen her since. I cannae believe it myself. Right enough, they had their issues but murder? And like that? No, it's just no' like Patricia."

"That's what I thought, but you know, I don't really know her at all. The more time I have spent with her recently, the more I just felt that it couldn't be her, even when..." Jessica tailed off, not quite ready to share the knowledge she had about Patricia's secretive phone call and the long, sorry saga about Helen Wilcott either – she didn't know how much Ealisaid knew, and it would have felt like breaking a confidence, even if Ealisaid was a good friend.

She picked up again, keen to establish the facts. "I mean, I was just thinking – the police must have something else, surely. Something more to go on that they had already, information that we don't have…" She stopped. Ealisaid was looking at her oddly.

"Have you not heard?"

"Heard what?"

"They found poison. At least that's what everyone is saying. They found it hidden in the Wilcotts' house. I think that's what led to the arrest – IF she's been arrested. Once again, I've only heard that here."

Ealisaid gestured towards the crowd of women clustered even more unevenly around the enlarged table. Jessica looked over. They had moved on from maligning Patricia Wilcott's name and settled in to the more familiar routine of sucking up to Margaret Mustard.

"How ANYONE could even have suspected you for a minute Margaret, it would have been an absolute travesty if they had pursued that line of questioning!" This was Miss Janet Simpson again, speaking forcefully over the babble of the assorted women, ensuring that she was heard.

"A miscarriage of justice!" said another.

"False accusation, or possibly police harassment." A third woman nodded sagely.

Margaret Mustard basked in the adoration, sitting smugly amongst her group. All the strain that Jessica had witnessed there over the last few days had gone – not a trace left. She looked relaxed and happy, happier than was perhaps appropriate in the wake of one man's death and his wife's subsequent arrest. Jessica felt an active dislike for the woman grow within her, and, not wanting to lose her temper in front of Ealisaid and the whole coffee shop, decided that it was time to get some air.

"I'm going to head over to Reenie's. She will have seen all the hustle and bustle here and be wondering what it is all about."

"Aye, no bother, Jessica. If I'm still here when she locks up, do pop in. I reckon I will be – this lot don't look like shifting any time soon."

Jessica nodded and headed out the door. She was looking both ways before crossing over the High Street towards The Bloom Room when she felt the hand on her arm. "Jessica...isn't it?"

The woman spoke hesitantly. A light breeze ruffled her silvery curls, and she was wearing the same long patterned green raincoat she had been wearing the other evening when Ealisaid and Jessica had briefly crossed paths with her when leaving the Wilcotts' house.

"Yes, that's right. You're a friend of Patricia's?"

"Yes, I'm Lillian. We met at Patricia's on Sunday evening. Can I have a moment?"

"Of course." Jessica stood back from the edge of the sidewalk. She could go over to Reenie's any time.

"I heard what they were all saying in there. There's a lot of confusion, but I know what it's like around here. There's no point trying to clear it up. I would just add to it, and the story would grow even more arms and legs."

Jessica allowed herself a half-smile at the unfamiliar expression. Lillian continued:

"I spoke to Patricia earlier after her interview with the police. She hasn't been formally arrested or charged. She is just 'helping the police with their enquiries', which still isn't great, I'll grant you, but it's not as bad as they are saying."

Jessica felt relief wash over her. "So that's all just gossip? They didn't find poison in her house?"

Lillian looked solemn.

"No, I'm afraid that's true. They did find a vial or something, I'm not sure of the details. I just know that Patricia was clearing away some trophies and things, and found it inside one of them. It was unfamiliar so she contacted the police and now they are asking her all sorts of more detailed questions. She seemed calm enough – you know Patricia, it takes a lot to rattle her, but it seems pretty serious in my opinion."

Jessica was stunned. In a trophy? She racked her brains to remember the various awards on the Wilcotts' mantel, knowing that the majority of them had been models of golfers swinging clubs mounted on plinths, or engraved shield shapes. She couldn't be one hundred percent sure, but she thought that the only one that could possibly contain something was the double-handled cup on display in the centre.

The one that she had picked up and examined, and that had definitely been empty on Sunday evening.

Lillian was still speaking. "She's fond of you Jessica, and I'm not sure if there's anything you can do, but I knew you were a reporter and that you had some experience of investigating things…can you help Patricia?"

Jessica looked at her directly. When she answered, she meant it with her whole heart. "I'll do what I can."

Lillian left, clearly reassured.

"What is all that about across the street?" Reenie looked up as Jessica entered The Bloom Room. She was alone, a customer having exited just as Jessica walked in. Willow bounded up to her, and this time didn't jump but just moved around her legs, her tail waving enthusiastically as she greeted one of her favourite humans.

"Everyone in *Lissa's* is talking about Patricia Wilcott's arrest. Except that she hasn't actually been arrested. Her friend just told me that outside. It isn't good though, Reenie."

"I wondered. Ealisaid is usually closing up by now, her crowd dies down in the afternoon. I knew something must have happened. Never a dull moment in Dalkinchie, is there! Life here can't be what you expected, Jessie." No-one but Reenie and her mom ever called her by this nickname, which Jessica considered childish. She didn't mind it from her aunt though - it was a nice reminder of home and family.

"It's probably not what I expected. It's more...real. I definitely had a romantic notion of life in a Scottish village! But in many ways it's so much better than I expected. It's hard to explain."

Reenie smiled at her niece. "No, you've explained it very well. It makes perfect sense. In a small community, you make connections quickly. Somebody's misfortune is everyone's misfortune. It can be stifling, but also quite wonderful to know that there are people around you who have your back. Take Patricia Wilcott. Here you are, helping her out, and a week ago you didn't even know her name."

"I wish I could help out. I don't know who killed her husband, and the one lead I thought I did have probably is just a dead end." Jessica was forlorn, thinking of how difficult it had been the day before trying to match old houses to the rough sketch she had on a piece of paper. There was no knowing how accurate that little sketch had been in the first place. Perhaps the MacNaughton's records would hold some vital information, but that would all take some time, and did Patricia Wilcott have any? She sighed.

"Right, Jessie. Here, can you take Willow and wait for me outside? I'm going to quickly mop and it's easier if she's no' here chasing it! Then we will head over the road and see if Ealisaid could use any help closing up, seeing as she's late tonight. We will put our heads together, go through everything we know and make a plan. I know you'll not rest until you help Mrs Wilcott out."

Reenie's tone was kind but firm, and Jessica was grateful. No point in being despondent. She did as she was requested and in no time at all they were crossing the road to *Lissa's* where they could see that Ealisaid had successfully got rid of her crowds, but was now facing the clear up alone.

"Need any help?"

Ealisaid looked up and a smile began to make its way across her elfin face.

"I would love that Jessica, thank you. Gets me home a little bit quicker! Can you make a start on clearing the tables?"

Reenie helped too, having successfully managed to occupy Willow with a chew beside the front door. As they worked they talked over Patricia Wilcott's case. "I told you not to trust the local gossip. They always exaggerate." Ealisaid was vigorously wiping down the counter and all the equipment.

"And you were right. However, she is under suspicion because of the poison found in her trophy. Ealisaid, can you remember what the trophies were like on the mantel? I can only remember one cup shaped one that could actually hold something."

"I don't, I'm afraid. I just remember a big jumble of silver. I've seen it every time I visited, but never paid close attention. What does it matter which trophy it was?"

"It matters because I picked that one up and it was empty on Sunday night."

"So if it *was* that trophy...whoever put it there did so after Sunday night? A visitor?" Reenie straightened up and paused from her sweeping. She cupped her hands over the top of the broom, and rested her chin on them.

"Exactly. Although I'm not one hundred percent sure about

the trophies. There could have been another one shaped like a cup. I don't remember it though." Jessica narrowed her eyes as she tried to recall the mantle. "I would need to go back to check – although apparently they have been cleared up. Or ask Patricia herself. I could also ask about the visitors she has had. Do either of you have her number?"

Reenie shook her head. Ealisaid didn't either, she had only had Desmond Wilcott's.

"Her landline number might be on the directory? You can search it online."

"OK, I could try that."

Reenie spoke up. "But if it was Patricia herself, she could have put it there whenever she liked – or not at all, and just claimed that's where she found it. It would seem a plausible place for a visitor to pop something in, and she's a clever woman, she knows that. You might have to consider that possibility, Jessie."

"True. I'd have to be careful how I asked her. If she claimed it was there then I'd know she was lying. I really don't think it's her though."

"Why are you so certain, Jessica? Do you suspect someone else? Or do you know something about Patricia that makes you think she is definitely innocent?"

Jessica took a deep breath. It was probably time to tell all.

"Honestly, it's just my feeling. I do know a few things but I think they probably point to her being more guilty, not less! I don't know though. I would wonder if she would risk it." Jessica told Reenie and Ealisaid everything she knew about Helen Wilcott and her relationship struggles in Australia, and the lengths Patricia had been going to to sort it out. She had wondered if this was common local knowledge but it seemed not. Ealisaid hadn't heard any of it before.

"Oh dear goodness, what a shame. What a difficult, difficult situation."

Reenie's feelings chimed with Jessica's, nothing but sympathy. Ealisaid was more pragmatic. "I wonder if the police know that she had already booked solo travel to Australia! That doesnae look good at all, Jess. Why on earth would she do that?"

Jessica didn't really have an explanation for that one.

"Well…she did tell me that her son-in-law and Mr Wilcott didn't get on. Maybe they felt, with the situation so delicate, it would be best to avoid upsetting him any more and Mrs Wilcott just travel alone? Or maybe he just didn't want to go?" She was aware she was clutching at straws.

Ealisaid still looked unconvinced. "Aye ok. That's possible I suppose. Who else is there though, Jess? Who else had it in for Desmond Wilcott to the extent that they would poison the marmalade? I know you think Patricia Wilcott is innocent – so if not her, who did it? What's your opinion?"

This was where Jessica fell down. She felt as hopeless as DI Gordon had on Monday, facing a hall full of people who potentially had access to the marmalade, and a man with a history of rubbing people up the wrong way. It would perhaps be easier to start with who didn't want to murder Desmond Wilcott.

Jessica remembered something she had seen at the Hall on the day of the Show. "I did see something – a marked up entry list, and it looked like it was in Mr Wilcott's handwriting. There were notes beside some entry numbers, and I can't be sure, but he could have been rigging the results."

Ealisaid nodded. "That's not surprising. I never caught him, but a few people suspected. It disnae seem like a murder motive, though."

147

Reenie, now mopping, paused again. "Yes, I think it would be something more personal."

"Well...what about Margaret Mustard then," said Jessica. "Her son lost his job."

"I thought she was exonerated?" Reenie replied.

"Not entirely. I mean, her marmalade wasn't poisoned at the Castle, not unless she was willing to risk poisoning the Laird of Drummond as well! But she had the same access to the hall that anyone else did that morning. She was there. She had a grudge against Desmond Wilcott – a big grudge. I think she's got to be considered.

"And then...well, there's you and I, Ealisaid. We had access to the marmalade jar alone, when nobody else did. I'm surprised the police haven't been a bit more suspicious! I suppose the fact that we were together the whole time until we locked the door means that we are each other's alibis?"

Ealisaid chuckled. "Plus, no motive! Unless you have a deep dark secret you're no' telling me? No, Desmond could be a tricky man but he wis basically decent. At least, I think so. The things you find oot later – well, I never had any problems with him, and he seemed happy enough to work alongside me.

"Plus, if I wis going to murder him, I would have waited until after the Show! The amount of work I've had to do – aye, it's amazing that I'm still standing."

Jessica laughed, but internally she wondered. She was increasingly suspicious of Margaret Mustard , and resolved to find out what she had been doing at the trash can in the park.

Plus, she really wanted to speak to Patricia again herself.

12

An Awkward Encounter

Jessica made her way into Dalkinchie High Street after her early morning walk down the dark, winding lanes of the park. When she reached the trash can she was sure Margaret Mustard had used, it was empty. She reached right down into the can to make sure. Definitely nothing there.

Disappointed, she walked a little further on to check that she was definitely in the right spot, but only found one further empty trash can. The evidence, if it had been evidence, was long gone. She would have to find another way to work out what had happened. Time for part two of her plan.

The day was cooler today, a stiff breeze sweeping down the wind tunnel of the High Street. Jessica had brought a raincoat of her own this morning, because Reenie had said that it was threatening rain. It had been a long, warm summer in Dalkinchie, and she had only had to wear it once before. Now, as she looked at the steel grey sky and the scudding clouds across it, she was glad that she had it with her.

Dalkinchie was still charming though, even when the weather

wasn't. The picturesque High Street boasting its many independent shops still give her a lot of pleasure after two months living in Scotland. She knew that Donald Donaldson's law firm had its offices in the High Street, and her plan was simply to start at one end and walk slowly down, taking a good look at all the buildings as she passed. She could have looked up the address, but both the walk and the exploration appealed to her.

She started at the Village Hall with the library, museum and her own office next to it. Moving down the High Street past Gillespie's restaurant, Jessica saw again the little cobbled nooks and crannies that Dalkinchie High Street was known for. During the summer, the High Street had been a riot of colour, with hanging baskets and colourful planters full of blooms. She paid careful attention to door signs and street numbers as she walked, and soon found a little brass plaque engraved with 'Donaldson's Family Solicitors and Attorneys at Law LLP'.

The adjacent door opened inwards and Jessica followed a short flight of stairs upwards to a half-landing where she continued on to the second floor offices of Donald Donaldson's practice. Here, the stairs opened out on to an upper floor gallery area. It was plush, carpeted in a tartan pattern with several large pot plants – real, Jessica noted – and a checked two-seater sofa placed beside the bannister with a small occasional table beside it. On the table, brochures and magazines were arranged in a fan shape. There was a door bearing a polished brass plate marked 'Secretary', and two further doors along the corridor, as far as Jessica could see.

Now that she was here, she wished she had changed into something more suitable – not that she had anything much with her in Scotland other than the jeans she was wearing today. Oh well, it wasn't worth worrying about now. She moved to the first door and gave it a gentle tap. Immediately from within a voice answered, "Come in!"

Jessica turned the brass doorknob and eased the heavy door inwards. It opened into a large square office with a rectangular desk directly opposite the door. Everything seemed carved from heavy dark wood, and here the carpet was still soft and expensive, but striped instead of tartan. Behind the desk sat a figure, framed by the light that streamed in from the window directly behind her. For a moment Jessica was discombobulated by the silhouette, unable to see her properly. As Jessica's eyes adjusted she first saw a neat bun, and then the face of a middle aged woman, eyebrows raised questioningly. As her sight further resolved she took in more about the woman who was wearing a collared shirt with an ornate brooch at the neck, and neat stud earrings.

Jessica made her way hesitantly into the room.

"Good morning," the woman said. "Do you have an appointment?" As she spoke, she drew a large leather bound appointment diary towards her, and flipped it open efficiently, using the silk marker in the book. She had been writing something when Jessica entered, and now used the pen to scan down the list of days and appointments. When she found no record of anyone due at this moment, she looked up, questioning.

Jessica hastened to reply: "No, I just came in hoping I might be able to speak to Mr Donaldson. It's regarding a friend of his. Do you think – would he be available to speak to me?"

The woman pursed her lips and shook her head slightly, glancing over the day's meetings. "Normally we would insist on an appointment. However, I can see that Mr Donaldson is not very busy today, and he might be willing to fit you in. Can

I have your name please, Miss – ?"

"Sure. It's Jessica Greer. I have met Mr Donaldson, a couple times actually, and it's about Patricia Wilcott. They are friends."

"Thank you."

If Donald Donaldson's secretary thought that this would make it more likely that Mr Donaldson would see her, she and her professional demeanour did not give anything away. Instead, she picked up the receiver of the telephone on her desk, and pressed a single button. When the connection was made at the other end, she stated the facts simply: "I have a Miss Greer here hoping to see you, Mr Donaldson. She doesn't have an appointment, however I have reviewed your diary for the rest of the day, and I think you should be able to accommodate her briefly unless you have something more pressing."

Jessica waited. The secretary nodded. A couple of 'mm-hmms', and then she said:

"Yes, I will let her know. One moment."

She replaced the receiver, and looked up at Jessica and smiled – a genuine, if taut smile. "You are in luck, Mr Donaldson feels he has time for a short appointment today. If you give me a moment I will show you through. Please just take a seat out in the waiting area, and I will be right with you."

The woman smiled at Jessica but made no move. Jessica thanked her, and stepped back out to the waiting area, closing the office door before taking a seat on the sofa.

She glanced to her side at the magazines on the table. Most of them seemed aimed at people whose life circumstances were very different to her own: people who took cruises, who needed to make elaborate life insurance plans, or who were looking to 'plan their estates' whatever that meant. Briefly her mind wandered into imagining a Scottish country estate with stables, gardens, maybe a walled garden. A fountain. A building a bit like Castle Drummond but with more turrets. Perhaps, why not, an orangery, although she only had the vaguest idea what one was – some sort of conservatory maybe? Was that what 'estate planning' meant? Were there really enough people with land and property like this for Donaldson Family Solicitors to make a viable living?

Around five minutes later, the woman emerged from her office and nodded to Jessica. She was carrying a polished black leather folder. She motioned for Jessica to follow her down the corridor to the farther away of the two doors, which she knocked and entered straight away.

"Mr Donaldson, the papers you required. I'll start work on the remaining ones immediately. Here is Miss Greer as discussed. Please let me know if you require any refreshments." As she spoke she smoothly slid a sheaf of closely printed A4 pages from the folder and placed them neatly on the corner of the desk within. Everything was precise, squared off, aligned.

She withdrew from the room.

"Miss Greer!" Donald Donaldson's welcome was hearty, and he got up from behind his own solid wooden desk and walked towards her with his hand outstretched, then vigorously shook hers. His hand was clammy, but also cool. "Do take a seat." He drew the chair out slightly and gestured.

Jessica sat down on the padded chair, shifting uncomfortably. She started by placing her hands on the desk but then moved them to her lap, loosely clasped. "Mr Donaldson, thank you for agreeing to see me this morning. I know that you are close friends with Patricia Wilcott. I heard yesterday of some...developments in her case? And I was wondering if you knew of anything I could do to help Patricia, or any way I might…"

Jessica trailed off. Now that she was here, in Donald Donaldson's office, this didn't seem like such a good plan. The solid weight of the heavy wooden furniture in the office, the sheer respectability and gravitas of their surroundings – it all made her and her theories feel and seem a little ridiculous. Who did she think she was, some sort of super-sleuth? The lined bookshelves, the sturdy and sensible looking rubber plant in the corner, the Roman blinds hanging in the sash windows, these were all the trappings of professionalism and success. What did she have, beyond an overactive imagination and a few wildcat theories? She glanced down at her hands, suddenly conscious of her chewed fingernails. And now, she noticed further, a slight grubbiness to one leg of her jeans, in the faded yet distinct mark of a paw print. Willow.

Donald Donaldson was still standing, leaning on the edge of the desk as he replied. "Patricia, yes, of course. I met you at her house at the weekend. A terrible business, terrible indeed. I'm not sure how you believe you can help, however? What assistance could you give? I'm sure Patricia is grateful for your support, but the matter is being handled by the police now, and I believe that's the best thing for it. I have confidence that they will sort the matter out, no matter how unpleasant, and I am unsure whether your *involvement* can be of much use. And obviously, as a friend of the Wilcotts and with a professional connection too, I am very limited as to what I can say. Very limited indeed."

Jessica wondered what he meant by "unpleasant". Did he, too, suspect Patricia? As her solicitor, she assumed he was up-to-date with the case.

"Well, you see, there's been a lot of talk – "

"Oh, I wouldn't pay any attention to idle gossip!"

Jessica flushed. No, perhaps she shouldn't have. She began to feel as if she had made a terrible mistake. She was out of her depth here, a silly little girl who didn't know anything. There was nothing to be gained by believing local stories.

"I'm sorry, Mr Donaldson. You are totally right. I shouldn't have listened. It's just that Patricia and I had breakfast yesterday morning, and she told me about what's been happening, and I wondered – "

Donald Donaldson splayed out his hands and began to move back behind the desk. He took his own seat opposite Jessica, and looked quizzically at her across the large leather inlaid surface. "Well as you're here, Miss Greer, I suppose there's no harm in you filling me in. I should know what's been said locally, and certainly everyone clams up when they see me coming! How did you find Patricia, yesterday?"

Still stinging from his earlier dismissal, Jessica was grateful for the apparent change of heart and thought back to their time in the cafe. "She was in quite good spirits I thought, considering," Jessica, remembering Patricia's demeanour earlier the day before, tried her best to convey it to Donald Donaldson.

"Considering her husband's death? Yes, well, as you've no doubt picked up for yourself, Desmond and Patricia didn't always have the happiest of relationships. I'm certainly not saying that she would have wished him dead – I'm not saying that at all – but I do believe that now he's gone, she's feeling some…freedom, I suppose is the best way to put it. There is no harm in saying that, it's just the truth of the matter."

Jessica considered his words. Had she picked up on this on Sunday evening at the Wilcott house? Perhaps. However, it wasn't exactly what she had meant.

"Erm...I was actually talking about her daughter, and all the trouble she is having coming to the U.K. But I agree with you, Patricia seems to be coping well with her husband's death although she's obviously shocked and upset. But yesterday it seemed as if it was her daughter's situation that was on her mind and now, being under suspicion with the poison being found in her house, well it just must all be – "

Donald Donaldson leaned forward, cutting her short. "Can I just stop you there Miss Greer. The situation with Helen Wilcott, you say...And something about poison?"

Jessica realised that she wasn't being clear. Her thoughts were muddled. The two things weren't connected, of course. Once again, she had the feeling of displacement, a 'silly wee lassie' putting her thoughts and theories where they weren't needed. She took a breath and started again: "Patricia told me about Helen when I had breakfast with her yesterday morning. Then, late yesterday afternoon, I heard that...something had been found in Patricia's house, and that it may have been involved in the death of Desmond Wilcott. No one seems exactly sure what happened, but I thought I might be able to throw some light on the situation, and I wanted to speak directly to Patricia if possible, to find out where it was discovered."

Donald Donaldson looked grave. Then he spoke up: "Patricia must really have trusted you to tell you the situation about Helen. I didn't realise you had grown quite so close. I must say, that's one of the things that really does make the case against her look quite bad." He shook his head.

Jessica didn't understand. Was he also aware of the single plane ticket to Australia? Was it the case, in fact, that Patricia knew she would be travelling alone because she had planned the death of her husband? Could that really be what Donald

Donaldson was hinting?

"I'm not sure I know what you mean. Why do her daughter's problems have anything to do with her husband's murder?"

Donald Donaldson didn't immediately reply, looking at Jessica then turning his chair slightly to look out of the window. Then he stood up, and moved over to a heavy sideboard against the side wall.

"Let me get you a glass of water Miss Greer, and we will start again." He poured from a tall pitcher standing on a silver tray and handed the glass to Jessica before returning to his own side of the desk. Jessica drank about half of it quickly, only now realising that the stuffiness of the building had dehydrated her, and her mouth felt dry and sticky. Donald Donaldson waited until she had finished before speaking.

"What exactly did Patricia tell you about her daughter's situation?"

"Just that she and her husband had split up, and it was making it difficult to return to the U.K. because neither parent wanted their child with the other. Also, the little girl doesn't yet have a passport, as I understand it."

Donald Donaldson brought his fingers together lightly under his chin. He looked off to the side. "That's correct, insofar as it goes. It's not the whole story however." He sighed. "Right. Please understand that what am I about to tell you, I do as a friend of the Wilcotts and with the knowledge that your own relationship with Patricia is clearly more developed than I had originally realised.

"In addition to the moral support Helen receives from her parents, she has often received financial support as well. They have paid for certain items she wanted for the child, plus on one occasion they paid for her flight home for a holiday – this was before the child was born. Helen didn't have a well-paid job you see, and since the child she hasn't worked again. Since her problems with her husband began, and now their subsequent separation, Desmond had been reluctant to step into the role of provider. He was a conservative man, who believed in the commitment of marriage, and he very strongly felt that Helen should have tried harder with Mark, and that she had made the decision to move on too quickly. He didn't feel that getting involved with financial support was the right thing to do under these circumstances, and indeed he cancelled a planned trip that he and Patricia were going to make to visit.

"Patricia, naturally, disagreed. She wanted to give Helen all the help that she needed, and to fly out there straight away. It was a large bone of contention between them. Very large indeed." Donald Donaldson had shifted his gaze as he spoke, and he was now looking directly at Jessica, the expression on his face unreadable.

Jessica was stunned; Patricia had not mentioned a word of this. Suddenly, it was clear why Patricia had rearranged her solo flight and done so in the privacy of the hall.

In the light of this new information that Donald Donaldson clearly saw as a potential motive, did Jessica believe that Patricia could have murdered her own husband? Patricia struck her as a clever woman, not one who would be stupid enough to book a solo flight and then feed her husband toxic marmalade on the same day.

And there was still the matter of the poison. Why would she tell the police about it, and say that she had found it? Surely that meant she was innocent? Particularly if, as Jessica suspected, it had been found in the trophy she had looked at, meaning that it had turned up after she had visited – after Sunday night.

She decided to tackle that. "It's true that I didn't know all that. I guess that's enough for a case against her? But that's why I wanted to speak to her – she can't have hidden the poison. I mean, the poison wasn't there!"

"What on earth do you mean Miss Greer? The poison wasn't there? Wasn't where?"

"I mean that if it's where I think it was, then it wasn't there on Sunday – oh it's complicated. I just really need to speak to her but I don't have a contact number. Would you be able to get a message to Patricia? It would be really good if we could meet and talk."

As Jessica spoke, the telephone on Donald Donaldson's desk gave two short rings and a button flashed red.

"That will be Marissa with my next appointment. Miss Greer, perhaps we should meet again, and you can explain more clearly what you mean by the poison – do you mean that you know what happened? I'm really quite unclear – "

Jessica, flustered, shook her head. "No, no. Please, if you can just pass on my number. I just have one question for Patricia, and then I'll understand more. Here, can I use this pen?"

She scribbled her cell phone number on a torn off piece of paper she had fished from her pocket and handed it across the desk to Donald Donaldson. "Just, please, tell Patricia I think I know something that might help. I'm really sorry to have taken your time Mr Donaldson. I'm grateful. Thank you."

"I'll do my very best to help out, Miss Greer, within certain limits of course. I'll make sure Patricia gets your message. Yes, indeed."

Jessica nodded and stood up, struggling slightly in her hurry to get out from between the desk and the chair. The heel of her sneaker caught in the thick plush of the patterned carpet as she backed away from the desk. Stumbling, she turned and bumped into Marissa who had silently come in the door holding another thick folder.

Embarrassed, she apologized and turned again to Donald Donaldson to check if he had noticed her awkwardness. Instead she found him fixedly staring, not at her, not at Marissa, but at something behind her shoulder. Jessica turned around and looked roughly in the direction of his gaze, but noticed nothing other than an old portrait beside the open door through which she now swiftly exited.

* * *

It took Jessica an hour to recover her scattered emotions. Luckily, the outer newspaper office was quiet today, and although Grant was in, he was both hard at work on something and understood that Jessica needed some time.

He really was the perfect boss, Jessica had begun to realize, her only previous employment experience being as a barista in a campus coffee shop. This had been fine, and she had enjoyed the camaraderie of having colleagues and the pleasure that comes with mastering new skills and delivering a good service, but as a bookish young woman with introverted tendencies, she and Grant had fallen into a companionable rhythm of working where they both could intuitively sense the other's need for focused time. Jessica used hers today to write up the previous day's primary school visit, the steady tapping of the keyboard and the sorting of her notes and impressions into logical paragraphs soothed and calmed her.

"Time for tea?" Jessica looked up. Grant was standing, tea already made, steam rising invitingly from a mug in each of his hands. Yes, truly the perfect boss.

"Yes please. I'm just coming to an end of this. Good timing!"

As was their habit, Grant and Jessica took their tea on the battered old leather sofa in the outer office.

"Are you still following the McScunnered leads, Jessica?"

"I don't know. Magnus and I were out of luck yesterday. And then when I came back here to the village, there was all that news about Patricia Wilcott's arrest and it kind of put it out my head. Did you hear?"

Even as she asked, Jessica knew what the answer would be. Although Grant Mack could not in any way be described as a gossip, his local connections and professional expertise meant he was as plugged in to local news as anyone could be. He would know about the developments in the case, and he would have heard from several different sources already. Jessica still could not believe the speed with which news travelled in Dalkinchie, and as the old saying said, the fastest of all was bad news.

"I did indeed. Quite a development, although as I understand it, initial reports of the arrest were perhaps a wee bit on the hasty side. Have you spoken to Patricia since?"

"No, I – " Jessica stopped herself. Just the thought of trying to describe what had happened in Donald Donaldson's office was enough to make the heat rise up in her cheeks again, and the resurgent panicky feeling of imposter syndrome. She wasn't ready to try and explain it to anyone yet, not even Grant. "No, I haven't. I don't have her number anyway, although I'm hoping she might try and get in touch with me." Jessica left it at that. The information she had received about the Wilcott's marriage had thrown her for a loop, and she was unsure whether she was quite so ready to continue to vouch for Patricia's innocence.

"I was asking about McScunnered because I have Nicholas

Pringle coming in shortly, and he is very well versed in local land, boundaries, conversions, zoning and so on – and the history as well. I'm not saying he will definitely be able to assist with identifying Abbotsford Farm, but if anyone local could help, he probably can. In any event, you are welcome to join us and ask some questions if you would like. I have yet to decide whether I will print the latest McScunnered letter next week – I held it back from the most recent issue. I feel there's enough of a question hanging over it to hold fire."

Jessica nodded. There could be no harm in hearing what Nicholas Pringle had to say.

In the event, he was late for his appointment with Grant, and Jessica was already getting ready to head down to *Lissa's* for her lunch, meaning that she only had the briefest of exchanges with him as they crossed paths in the stairwell.

"Miss Greer! The gaffer in, is he?"

The shirt was blue today, and his pants a sickly mustard colour, but the man was as eye-catching as ever.

"Hello, Mr Pringle. Grant's waiting for you in the office."

"Thank you."

Jessica continued down the stairs. With events overtaking the case the way they had, she too no longer felt that the pursuit of McScunnered was a priority.

* * *

It was a relief to head to *Lissa's* for lunch. That is, it was a relief until Ealisaid spoke. "Jessica! I've a message from Murdo and DI Gordon for you. Give me a wee minute and I'll pass it on."

Ealisaid no longer had to ask for Jessica's order. She had automatically began to prepare her regular latte as soon as she spotted her through the window, and handed it directly to her friend as soon as she reached the top of the line. Jessica took the mug and placed it on her customary table closest to the counter, hooking her backpack over one of the chairs. She knew that Ealisaid would follow up the coffee with a grilled cheese sandwich, or 'toastie' as it was known in Scotland. This small thing – a regular lunch order at a local coffee shop – was one of the many and varied reasons that Scotland in general, and Dalkinchie in particular, was beginning to feel more and more like home for Jessica. She waited until the line behind her had cleared and went back up to the counter to speak to Ealisaid.

"You said you have a message for me? Are the police looking for me?" As she spoke a jolt of adrenaline to her stomach made Jessica realise that she had not, in fact, completely recovered from her earlier experience in Donald Donaldson's offices. She was instantly on the alert again, feeling the flush creep up her cheeks. What was the cause of this uncomfortable feeling? She had nothing to hide!

Ealisaid, steel milk jug in one hand, the other on her green tartan apron-clad hip, smiled with amusement at her friend. "Well. Not exactly. You are not the subject of an international manhunt or anything like that! I just mean they were in anyway for coffees and cakes but they asked if you were about, and to say that if I saw you, could you go up to the Hall and have a wee chat."

What now? Jessica wondered to herself. It wasn't as if she had shared any information about her own suspicions with anyone. DI Gordon had told her to leave the McScunnered leads alone, and he had been right, tempting as it was – she was looking no further. They couldn't have known that she had been to see Donald Donaldson, could they? Had he been in touch with them? What could he have told them? She hadn't spoken a word of the overheard phone conversation to anyone apart from Reenie and Ealisaid, but in the light of further information she had begun to wonder whether it was significant enough to tell the police. Would it be seen as covering up if she didn't?

Jessica took a deep breath. She was getting paranoid. "Can I take the toastie to go, please Ealisaid? I guess I had better head up there right now and find out what they want. Murdo didn't tell you?" She hoped that his customary loose-lippedness might have given a clue to what was going on.

"Surprisingly, he did not. And there was something else I was going to ask you as well. Give me a wee minute while I remember what it was. In fact, give me back your coffee and I'll put it in my own cup for you to take out." Jessica retrieved her latte from where it had been awaiting her on the table, and Ealisaid expertly poured it into a reusable takeaway cup. She glanced at Jessica as she did so. "You need to get yourself one of these Jessica…I'm going to start offering rewards to people who bring in reusable cups. Anyway, I have remembered what I was going to ask. What are you doing on Friday night?"

"This Friday?" Jessica didn't really have to think about it. Even during her student days she had never been big on Friday nights out, and now in Dalkinchie her life had settled into occasional drinks at the local pub with either Reenie or Ealisaid and once, particularly memorably, a delicious meal out for Reenie's birthday at Gillespie's, Dalkinchie's fine dining establishment where she had eaten wild salmon and locally grown potatoes. She still savored that memory.

"Not a thing, apart from whatever you are going to ask me to do!" She smiled widely at her friend.

Ealisaid smiled back. "Good, that's what I was hoping you would say. Hear me out though, before you agree to this. It's a little weird."

"Okay, now you've got me intrigued."

Ealisaid followed up. "I have had an outside catering job booked for a while. It's at the Golf Club, and it's a sort of an award ceremony for the Donaldson cup winner." Her eyes searched Jessica's face for any sign of the penny dropping. She wasn't disappointed.

"The Donaldson cup...that's the one that Desmond Wilcott won this year?"

"He won it more than just this year, Jessica. In fact it was the tenth time in a row that he had won it, and as a celebration they commissioned a portrait to be painted and hung in the clubhouse with all the other celebrated golfy men of Drummond and Dalkinchie. It was to be this Friday evening, and I contacted them yesterday to check what they wanted to do, assuming that they would be canceling. Turned out I was wrong – they are going ahead with the event and with the unveiling, although now it's going to be a memorial rather than a celebration. So I'm still needed; and I could do with help with setting up, serving drinks and so on. It's a buffet, so no serving food, should be pretty easy once it's running. Just wine, orange juice and water, they can go to the bar for anything stronger."

Jessica took this in. "Will Patricia be there?'

"I should think so, provided she hasn't been chucked in jail by then!"

Jessica knew Ealisaid and her sense of humour well enough not to take this too seriously. "Count me in. I'll definitely help. Just tell me when and where to turn up and I'll be there!"

"That's wonderful, Jessica. I really do need the extra pair of hands, and I'm assuming that Murdo will no' be available now. This is the first time they've hired me at the Golf Club and I'm hoping to impress them – I'd love to get more work there, lots of people wi' money who might be throwing their own parties and in need of a caterer! I'll be handing out cards, that's for sure."

Jessica wasn't going to miss the chance to speak to Patricia, even if she had to wait two days to do it, especially when as a bonus she could help out a good friend at the same time.

She would rather do it sooner, though. A lot could happen in two days.

13

A Bit Hingy

"You cannae put that there!"

DI Gordon looked around helplessly as his coffee cup was removed from his grasp and sailed away behind his right ear. He instinctively began to apologize without really being clear what his crime was.

"Aye, well, that's one of our wooden tables. If ye start sticking your coffee mugs on it, you'll likely mark it. You can do that on they other tables, they just have a vinyl finish, but no' these ones. They were original from back when the Hall was built and we dinnae want them ruined. I'll away and get you a coaster. I'll get you a wee plate for your cakes as well while I'm at it."

"We're awfy sorry, Mrs Menzies. We'll no' do it again." Murdo, not yet seated, placated the caretaker, taking the DI's coffee cup from her hand. He towered over her by at least a foot, and despite the air of authority his Special Constable police uniform gave him, anyone watching the scene would be in no doubt that the diminutive woman in dark green overalls was in total charge of the situation. She bustled away, Murdo following behind her offering to help out.

"Och, you're fine Murdo laddie – I dinnae need any help with a couple of coasters and a plate or two! You can scrub the floor in the main hall if you want – no, didnae think that would appeal to you." Clearly mollified by his offer, Sheila Menzies twinkled at the young man although it didn't stop her muttering to herself as she shuffled towards the door of the small room. "Over a hundred years old those tables...they'll no' be damaged on my watch! Honestly, you'd think people had forgotten that coasters existed these days...it's no' them that would have to get the french polishing done..."

DI Gordon rolled his eyes at Murdo, but if he had been expecting any solidarity there he was disappointed. Murdo, loyal as ever, was firmly backing up Mrs Menzies' stance. "She's no wrong, it can be a right pain in the bahookie to try and get cup rings oot of polished wood. My wee granny told me that, there was a mark on her old press once and she said you could try salt and bicarb, although that's a wee bit rough so you'd have to go very gently and use a soft cloth, or you can do lemon oil I think but I dinnae know where you would get that, or she even said she'd heard tell of mayonnaise mixed wi' ashes but she didnae like mayonnaise you see, she always preferred salad cream so that wis a no go – plenty of ashes, right enough, she always enjoyed a proper wood fire..."

The Detective Inspector waited as patiently as he could. He was beginning to learn that there was no point in interrupting Murdo in full flow, and anyway, today he felt particularly tired and just not up to the task. He and his partner had recently welcomed twins to their family, and the broken nights were beginning to take a heavy toll. They had been repeatedly told that it would 'get better', but for a man who liked precision, procedure and predictability this offered little reassurance. No-one seemed willing to offer a detailed timeline. When exactly would they sleep through the night? He yawned.

Murdo was drawing to a close. " – and she never smoked again, just like that. Cold turkey. I wonder why they call it that? What's cold about a turkey? – "

This time DI Gordon did think he should intervene, before Murdo could start on a whole new cycle. Luckily there was no need, as Mrs Menzies returned to the room, cutting off this new train of thought. She was carrying the promised coasters and plates, but also, over one arm, a neatly folded and pressed snowy white tablecloth.

"I jist thought that it would be a bit nicer if you had it made up properly. Shift oot the way there, would you." Mrs Menzies used her free arm to unceremoniously brush DI Gordon's notes to the edge of the table where he quickly grabbed them before they slid off completely, and she shook out the tablecloth with a quick one-handed flick, letting it settle smoothly over the length of the table.

"We really don't need – " this was fruitless. DI Gordon may as well not have spoken.

"Well now, that's a bit better, isn't it." As she spoke Sheila Menzies deftly set out the coasters and placed the coffee mugs on them. In a trice, the cakes were unboxed and presented on the floral plate, with two smaller plates laid in front of the men. DI Gordon began to wonder if he was in fact dreaming. Was he working, or was he out for afternoon tea? Pulling himself together, he thanked the caretaker, who nodded. He wasn't completely forgiven, however. "Well, it's just as I say, those are old tables, and just a few wee touches will protect them for the future, last another 100 years they will, dinnae fancy trying to get cup rings oot of wood today, I've the Brownies starting back after school and need to get the big Hall set up and I'd never gie them the wooden tables, not wi' all the glitter and glue they use..."

Off she went.

All James Gordon had wanted was somewhere quiet in Dalkinchie to collect his thoughts and try to make some progress with this case. None of it made any sense to him at all. He tended to go back to first principles in times like this, but with this case that wasn't helping. Means – well, they had been advised that liquid nicotine was widely available to purchase now due to the rise of vaping, and there was nothing distinctive about the vial they had found. If that indeed was the murder weapon. Opportunity was a lost cause. The room had been locked, so really no-one had the opportunity. However, the keys were widely available, so in fact almost everyone had had the opportunity, although it would have taken some nerve. The Hall had had its busiest day all year and at least 150 people had been through its doors. It had been fruitless to try and narrow that down. Motive – the wife Patricia appeared to have the strongest motive, as was often the case, but why would she voluntarily draw their attention to the nicotine?

He couldn't make it make sense. Perhaps the forthcoming conversation with Jessica Greer would shed some light on the situation. James knew that the young woman had been the first person to meet Patricia Wilcott as she arrived at the Hall following her husband's collapse, and he wondered if she could have insights into her frame of mind or any action that had seemed out of place, or peculiar. It was a little unusual, and not routine, but he had been impressed by Jessica's prescience and persistence, and felt that she was in possession of a shrewd mind and some fine observational skills.

It couldn't hurt to have her take.

* * *

When Jessica arrived at the Village Hall, Mrs Menzies directed her towards the side room where DI Gordon and Murdo had set themselves up.

"Miss Greer." Once again, Jessica noticed how tired DI Gordon looked, and wondered what could be the cause. This case, while complicated, was surely pretty standard for him. She waited as he flipped open his notebook, frowned, moved it to one side, rubbed his eyes and then looked at her again.

"I was wondering if you had anything additional to tell us...ah...anything you might have noticed that was perhaps a little out of the ordinary? Perhaps with regards to Mrs Wilcott?"

Jessica froze. The way he had phrased the question sounded as if he knew that there was something she hadn't told him. Her mind flitted wildly back to the Saturday morning at the top of the stairs in the newspaper offices. There had been no one else there, she was sure of that. Patricia had not seen her, and hadn't mentioned it since. Even if the police knew that Patricia had rearranged her single flight just hours before her husband's death, there was simply no way they could know that Jessica knew that fact. She took a deep breath. Her nerves were still jangling and she was beginning to feel a little hot as well, although the weather outside was dry and cool. She glanced at the windows in the small room. Closed. Murdo's face gave nothing away, his expressive, open face wore its usual calm, happy expression.

James Gordon watched the young woman opposite him. His own words repeated themselves in his ear, hardly his most incisive questioning ever. Still, it would probably do the job since he wasn't really sure what he was asking for – he was just hoping that Jessica might present a fresh perspective on a case that was becoming stuck, without actually inviting her to join the force.

He suppressed a small shiver. It wasn't cold, he knew that – the August day outside was warmer than was typical for late Scottish summer, but sleeplessness seemed to have brought with it a lack of ability to regulate his own body temperature. He glanced at the windows in the small room. Already closed. Murdo's face gave no indication that he had an opinion about the phrasing of the question. He looked exactly the same as he always did, and as DI Gordon watched, he selected a cake from the plate on the table and began to eat it.

Jessica cleared her throat, which was suddenly feeling scratchy. "Nothing has been really ordinary, Detective Inspector...I mean, I have spoken to Patricia a couple of times and I think she's coping OK, but I haven't seen her since – " she interrupted herself, unsure how to phrase the next part of the sentence. Since she had been implicated in her own husband's death? Since she found the poison? Since her unfair arrest?

" – since yesterday morning." She finished, lamely. She swallowed. Still scratchy. She lifted Ealisaid's cup to her lips, but found it empty. There was no water on the table – although, as she now realized, it looked as if she had interrupted DI Gordon and Murdo in the middle of afternoon tea. A floral plate in the centre of the table held some of Ealisaid's finest delicacies and Murdo was, in fact, placidly finishing off a strawberry tart. Normally Jessica would have been quite envious – the little fruit and cream filled tarts were her favourites – but right now it didn't appeal at all. In fact, she realized, she was feeling a little queasy.

James Gordon was having trouble focusing on Jessica's words. All he could hear was the noise of Murdo eating the cake; chew, chew, slurp. Chew, chew, slurp. Chew, chew – how could the man take such a long time to eat such a tiny cake? Then, suddenly, the noise receded, to be replaced with an insistent ringing in his ears. Or was it buzzing? He blinked and realized that Jessica had stopped speaking and he had taken absolutely nothing from what she had said. The room suddenly seemed impossibly bright. His eyes were beginning to water. He opened his mouth to speak, although he had no idea what he was going to say, but before he could get a chance, Murdo interjected.

"You don't look very well, Jessica. You look a wee bit hingy. Are you sure you shouldnae be in your bed?"

A look of relief came over Jessica's face. "I actually do think I'm getting sick. Can we do this another time?"

Murdo glanced towards the Detective Inspector who nodded, and then the young Special Constable rose to his feet. "Come on then, I'll walk you hame. I think it's maybe a hot toddy and a cozy blanket that you need! There's been a few bugs going about, it's always the same when the schools go back. Up you get."

They departed from the room. James knew that he should be concerned about the young woman, and should probably try and follow them to make sure she was OK.

Instead, he just wanted to curl up and fall asleep.

* * *

Grateful for Murdo's company, Jessica made her way along the path towards the cottage. It was a good thing she had left when she did. All of a sudden she felt boiling hot. A fever, on top of everything else, perhaps? Her head ached, her throat was definitely actually hurting, and the toastie she had eaten – far too fast, she now realized – was sitting heavily in her delicate stomach. She hoped she could make it home before that was no longer the case.

Murdo, striding beside her, was chatting away comfortably. "As I say, there's quite a few wee bugs going about and you and Magnus were up at Drummond Primary, were you no'? Or maybe it was something you ate?"

Jessica's internal alarm system pinged. Apart from the toastie, what had she eaten that day? Her eyes swam. She focused on her feet, moving them one after the other, step, step, step along the path until finally the small bridge that signalled the start of the direct path to Reenie's cottage came into view.

"Do you need me to come in, Jessica?" Murdo seemed untroubled, so it couldn't be as bad as all that. He had taken her all the way to the door of the cottage.

"No, I'll be fine. I'll go straight to bed."

Murdo nodded and took his leave, walking back the same way they had come.

True to her word, Jessica managed only to take her shoes off before tumbling into her bed and falling in to a hot, bewildered sleep.

* * *

The room was still when she awoke, and for a moment Jessica was utterly confused. Unaccustomed to napping during the day, she couldn't understand why she was in bed while the light through the window told her that it could not be night time.

And why did her head feel like that?

She sat up as she remembered what had happened, testing her body to see where the trouble was. It all seem centred in her head, which felt like it might burst, although her limbs ached unbearably too, and – she now realized – her chest felt tight.

Jessica panicked, sitting there alone in her room, tears coming readily to her eyes. What could be wrong with her? With horror, she remembered the coffee she had left sitting unattended on a table in the café. How could she have been so stupid? She knew that there was a poisoner on the loose, and she didn't really believe it could be Patricia, which logically meant that it must be someone else – and she had left a drink sitting in full view of anyone in Dalkinchie who had happened to be in the café. Perhaps the true culprit knew she was investigating the murder? Who knows what might have been put into her drink? Was this how Desmond Wilcott had felt?

She had to contact Reenie. She managed a quick text before falling back into a feverish sleep.

When she next awoke, Reenie was sitting next to her bed. There was a tall glass of water sitting on the nightstand, and something cool spread across her head. The light had changed somewhat, the August evenings, while still summery, contained more than a hint of fall – autumn, as Reenie would say.

"Hey, there. How are you doing, Jessie?"

Jessica focused on her aunt's face. How was she doing? Once again she was unsure. She tried to sit up and Reenie eased the process by adjusting the pillows comfortably behind her as she rose. Jessica realised that she was feeling a little better. The intense pressure in her head had lessened, although her throat was still hurting when she swallowed. She didn't feel quite as hot either, and her heart rate had slowed down to a level she could cope with.

"Reenie. I'm so sorry, I don't know what's wrong with me…I feel so sick."

Reenie gently stroked her niece's brow.

"I think you just have a virus, Jessie, but Grant is looking into you seeing a doctor. I've been so remiss, not getting you signed up sooner. There is an out-of-hours service, but we just need to work out how you access it as a visitor. Then we will get you an appointment."

"Grant's here?"

"Yes. He was in the shop when I got your message, and we came together. He's downstairs with Skye and Willow. Do you have a sore throat? I can make you a ginger tea, and put some honey in it if that sounds good?"

That sounded perfect, and Jessica said so. As Reenie went downstairs, she lay back in her pillows and contemplated what had happened. The fear of a few hours ago had faded somewhat, and she felt a little stupid for her earlier panic. Perhaps it really was just a virus.

A mug of sweet, spicy tea later, and Jessica felt well enough to go downstairs. She found Reenie sitting in front of the fireplace. Willow, clearly in a playful mood, kept jumping in front of Skye who had taken the coveted spot on the rug. The puppy barked and play-bowed, trying to entice Skye to get on her feet and run around with her. Skye raised her head and looked steadily at the puppy, then tucked it down again, lifting her eyes and looking pleadingly at Reenie, and as Jessica moved over, flicking her soulful gaze to her as well. Reenie picked up a tug toy and waved it in front of the pup, trying to distract her with a game. Jessica dropped into the armchair beside Skye.

"Jessica. It's good to see you up and about."

Grant had come through from the kitchen, wearing an apron tied around his waist. That explained the drifting smells of sautéed onions…and maybe sweet peppers? Jessica didn't feel hungry, but the fact that Grant was here, cooking for Reenie in her kitchen, was not lost on her. Maybe she was starting to feel better after all.

"Thanks, Grant, Honestly, I am beginning to feel like I overreacted a bit. I felt so, so sick earlier!"

"You were sleeping when we arrived, and hot but not worryingly so. Reenie thought it would be a good idea to bring down your temperature and try to get you a doctor's appointment."

"I feel much cooler now. I'm still not right, but I'm not as scared as I was earlier. I really thought – " Jessica didn't expand on what she had thought. It was embarrassing to admit that she had worried that she might have been poisoned.

"Well, we've established that you can just turn up at the out-of-hours doctors and they will schedule you, so if you think you need to do that we can. However, Reenie thinks it's probably the beginning of a nasty virus and I must say, I agree. The early stages can make you feel very ill. If your temperature is coming down then I would hope that you might find relief from the other symptoms quickly."

Jessica looked at Grant, standing there in his apron, oven glove flipped over his forearm. His head slightly tilted to the side, concern and – yes, affection, written all over his face. Reenie, still half-engaged with the tussle with Willow, had been nodding along while Grant spoke. Unexpected tears prickled the back of Jessica's eyes. She had been lucky enough to grow up in a close-knit, caring family, and here in Scotland it seemed that she had found the same again.

* * *

A good night's sleep improved Jessica's symptoms and her spirits even further, and a doctor had been ruled unnecessary. Despite this, Reenie had prescribed a day of rest and Grant had agreed. There was nothing pressing at the newspaper, he'd said, and it would be better if Jessica returned in full health rather than trying to battle through the symptoms and probably take longer to get better. She should rest.

This had sounded like a great plan, and Jessica did want to recover enough to help out Ealisaid at her outside catering job the following evening. The only problem? By midday, Jessica was bored. She had drifted around the cottage, done a little laundry, watched some daytime TV, read a couple of chapters of her book, and was now attempting to do a meditation exercise. One of her sisters had sent her the link.

Jessica sat crossed-legged on the rug, closed her eyes, pictured the calm beach scene as instructed, tried to relax her whole body...but felt her attention drifting within fifteen seconds, wondering whether Patricia would call her. She opened one eye and peeked at the screen of her cell phone. No messages. She sighed, and tried to tune in again to the woman's soporific voice. This time, it was only ten seconds before she began to wonder if it was too early for lunch.

Jessica wished that Reenie had at least left Willow behind to provide a little company and stimulation.

By early afternoon, Jessica knew that she had a heavy cold but was otherwise feeling a lot better. Reenie had left her some hot medicated lemon drinks to take and they had cleared her head and soothed her throat. Her appetite had recovered, and she was contemplating going into Dalkinchie village after all, when the noise of a car drawing up outside attracted her attention.

Glancing out the window, Jessica saw Patricia Wilcott emerge from her car, drawn neatly up to the sidewalk just outside Reenie's small front garden. The woman reached back in to her car to remove a bunch of flowers, walked smartly down the path and rapped a couple of times on the front door.

"Jessica, how are you feeling my dear? Your aunt said you had taken ill. Here, these are for you," Patricia said, proffering the flowers.

"That's so kind! Thank you. I'm actually feeling a lot better. Come in. When were you speaking to Reenie?"

"I have just come from her shop – these are from me, but she made them up with you in mind."

Jessica took the delicate bunch from her. Reenie knew her favorites, and had incorporated some sweet-smelling freesia.

"I hope you don't mind me popping in to see you. I had been wanting to catch up; I wasn't sure what you had heard, but there have been a number of developments since our breakfast the other day."

Jessica nodded. "I guess Mr Donaldson hasn't given you my message yet."

"I saw Donald this morning, but he didn't mention anything. What did you want to talk about?"

Jessica struggled with her next words. She didn't want to upset Patricia by hinting at the gossip that she had been hearing. But Patricia was pragmatic; and she put Jessica straight.

"I know what everyone is saying, Jessica. They think I have been arrested for poisoning my husband. I haven't, of course, or I wouldn't be standing here talking to you now. I found a vial of nicotine. A small glass thing, tucked away on my mantelpiece. I would never have found it if I hadn't been clearing those

179

trophies off the mantelpiece to pack away. All of a sudden I got tired of looking at a shelf full of his achievements, you know? It all felt meaningless and more than a little sad. What does a life amount to in the end?"

Patricia stopped, and pressed her lips together tightly for a moment, closing her eyes. She took a breath, and continued:

"We didn't always get on, Desmond and I, although we did build a marriage and a life together, and raised a wonderful daughter. As hard as things sometimes were, I'm proud of what we achieved and all that silver on the mantelpiece – it wasn't about that. I wanted them boxed up and away, and I had this sudden realization that I didn't have to ask anyone for permission so I went ahead and did it. That's when I found the nicotine. I told the police straight away, and naturally they had a lot of questions for me. That's all. I imagine whoever put it there wanted to frame me, but didn't count on me finding it first. I suppose I'm lucky the police didn't search my house!" The normally porcelain Patricia had a spot of high colour on each cheekbone. Jessica finally got her opportunity to get a word in edgeways, and question Patricia about the nicotine.

"Where was the nicotine vial exactly?"

Patricia looked confused. "Inside a trophy on the mantelpiece. I just told you."

"No, I mean which trophy exactly? Because I looked at them a bit on Sunday, and there aren't many that are like a cup, you know, that would hold something inside. A lot of them were shaped more like a shield."

"Oh yes, I see what you mean. It was the large one in the centre. The Donaldson one. It's got a deep bowl, perfect for concealing things. You wouldn't see anything unless you looked right inside, or picked it up and heard it rattle."

Jessica felt a jolt of excitement, She had been right.

"Then…Patricia, it wasn't there when I looked at it on Sunday! I did pick that one up and had a good look. I'm honestly sure…really, it was definitely empty. Whoever put it there…"

"Must have done so after Sunday, and before I found it on Tuesday afternoon." Patricia finished the sentence, looking at Jessica with widened eyes. Her next question took Jessica by surprise.

"Are you feeling well enough to go out?"

"Actually, yes. I am feeling a lot better. The paracetamol is helping. I was planning on going out. I'm getting really bored stuck in the house."

"Right. Come with me."

"Where are we going?"

Jessica could not have predicted the next words that came from Patricia's lips.

"We are going to confront my husband's murderer."

14

Margaret Mustard Speaks

Patricia had remained tight-lipped throughout the journey, driving efficiently around the curves and bends, and fobbing off Jessica's entreaties for more information. Soon it was evident where she was headed, as she took the unmistakable winding road up to the gates of Castle Drummond. Patricia walked determinedly across the gravel drive, round to the side door that Jessica had been through earlier in the week and knew led to the kitchen and pantry. Patricia gave it one smart rap and then, opening it before waiting for a response, strode straight through. A woman on a mission.

Margaret Mustard was bent over the large range stove at the far end of the large room, stirring a wooden spoon around a stock pot. She turned as the two women entered, her mouth falling open in a perfect round 'O' of shock.

"Margaret Mustard, how could you! I knew you hated him...but to go this far. And then to make it look as if it was me!"

Patricia didn't stop until she was inches from the woman, too close for comfort. Margaret was several inches taller, but was clearly intimidated by the shorter woman's fierce demeanour. Although as she began to speak, Jessica felt she was missing something entirely.

"Patricia, I dinnae know what to say…I'm so sorry, I never meant for any of it to happen!"

"I am not saying that he didn't hurt you Margaret, and I understand why you were angry at him. But this! And what do you have against me?"

After a brief silence, Patricia – to everyone's surprise, not least her own – burst into loud, noisy sobs. She backed away from Margaret and found a chair, dropping into it and continuing to cry. The adrenaline that had brought her all the way here from Dalkinchie, up the winding road and through the door had clearly deserted her. Gone was the composure she had maintained for nearly a week. Jessica rushed to her side and so did Margaret Mustard. The latter dropped to her knees beside Patricia and put a hand on her shoulder.

"Patricia, I'm so, so awfy sorry. I really never meant for things to end up like this. It was all a big mistake and I've been so worried, you'll never know, it's been keeping me up at night. There wis no love lost between me and your husband for sure, but I am not the sort of person who would do something like that. It has been a terrible, terrible time and I've felt so badly."

Margaret's words rang true and it would certainly explain her emotional reactions and furtive behavior over the past few days, but Jessica couldn't comprehend what she was hearing. How could mixing nicotine into a pot of marmalade be described as a mistake?

"I wish I had never entered my marmalade in the Show. All those years ago. I loved entering the knitting, but I had never entered the edible classes. My pal Janet suggested it, and all of a sudden, there I was, with my Orange & Whisky taking best in show! The pressure, you can't imagine. All of a sudden I had to keep up appearances and enter year after year, especially when I joined the committee of the Guild. I think they only took me because I was the marmalade winner. I wis so worried, every year, that this would be the time that I didnae win."

Patricia sniffed, watery eyes looking into Margaret's. "You needn't have worried about that Margaret. Desmond was many things, and a bit of a snob was one of them. As long as your Castle Drummond marmalade kept being entered, I can guarantee it would have won. He enjoyed the status of it, and he liked keeping the Laird sweet. I'm not saying your marmalade wasn't delicious, of course," Patricia added hastily. *Could she really be fearful of offending Margaret Mustard's marmalade?* Jessica wondered. It seemed a bit incongruous, following a murder accusation.

It seemed as if it might be too late. Tears were now brimming in the housekeeper's eyes and she pressed her trembling lips together to try and conceal her emotion. It didn't work. Jessica watched on, recognising that her contribution was not needed.

"Oh Patricia! The strain I have been under! It's too much." Margaret Mustard got stiffly to her feet. Jessica quickly pulled one of the other chairs out for her, and the woman nodded her thanks. "It's going to be such an enormous relief to finally tell the truth."

But before she could continue, the strident peal of a fire alarm blared out across the castle.

"My onions!"

Margaret dashed to the stove at the back of the room, Jessica in pursuit. Margaret quickly grabbed a cloth and moved the large pot from the hot plate to a cast iron pot stand on the side. Smoke billowed, and Margaret ran to open windows and the back door.

"What's all this? Are you all right, Margaret?"

Gillespie MacNaughton strode in through the interconnecting side door, resplendent as ever in his kilt. *Does he sleep in that thing* Jessica wondered, but in no time the MacNaughton had switched off the alarm, had a damp tea towel blanketing the offending pot, and was comforting Margaret.

"What on earth happened here, Margaret? It's no' like you to forget you've something on the hob!"

"Och I know, Gillespie. I just got distracted. Patricia and the wee lass that works for *The Herald* came over, and we were having a wee bit of a chat." Margaret gestured over to Jessica and Patricia as she spoke.

Patricia, having recovered herself somewhat, spoke firmly. "Actually, Mr MacNaughton, we were having more than just a 'wee chat.' Margaret was about to tell us how she had accidentally poisoned my husband!"

Gillespie MacNaughton looked at his housekeeper in horror. "Margaret! Surely no'. I thought we had all that sorted oot. I broke the jar that was meant to go into the Show, remember. Unless you poisoned the lot of them, but that would mean that you didnae mind poisoning me!" Gillespie MacNaughton guffawed loudly, but this was not reflected by Margaret Mustard's reaction, who was blinking furiously and biting her lip.

"Gillespie, I've something to tell you. I have something to tell you all. It's probably best if we all sit down.

"It's time I came clean."

* * *

DI Gordon sat hunched over the table in *Lissa's*. Feeling a little better than he had the day before, he still needed regular boosts of caffeine to get him through, and had therefore been grateful when Murdo said he needed to have a word with Ealisaid.

"Take all the time you need, Murdo!" he had said generously, before ordering an espresso and a Danish pastry, thinking that adding sugar to the mix couldn't hurt. Everyone said that the sugar rush was artificial, short lived and ended in a crash, but at this point he would take anything.

"So I cannae help oot at the service, although I will be there." Murdo's round blue eyes looked anxiously into Ealisaid's. He didn't like letting her down, although she had been nothing but supportive of his volunteer constabulary work. Daytimes were getting easier now that Mairead was old enough to do weekend shifts, and had plenty friends looking for a wee bit of extra cash. This outside catering gig had been booked for a while though, and Murdo had only just realized that there was a clash.

"I'm one step ahead of you, Murdo. I just assumed you'd be tied up, given that it's Desmond Wilcott's memorial, so I've asked Jessica to help me out tomorrow evening. She said aye, and although she's had a nasty bug apparently, she thinks she'll be ok to work by then. So I'll see you at Drummond Club House, but I'm no' expecting you to work – I'll be serving you instead!"

Murdo smiled in relief, and joined DI Gordon at his table. The Detective Inspector was sitting staring fixedly ahead. Murdo glanced around, but could see nothing. DI Gordon had been doing this lately, getting distracted. Murdo waved his hand gently in front of his superior's face.

"Hmmm? Oh – sorry, Murdo. I was miles away. Did you sort

things out with Ealisaid?"

"Aye. It's all fine, Jessica will take my catering shift, so I can come wi' you and Mrs Wilcott to the service."

DI Gordon yawned. "Thanks, Murdo. It's a bit of an ask, but we in the force do like to attend funerals and services if we can. It shows respect but in addition, it's often a good opportunity to spot if anyone is behaving oddly or shows an unusual reaction to events. With this case, I'd really like to see if anything new emerges."

He stopped short of saying that they were drawing a blank, but it was getting perilously close to it. If they didn't manage to get a case together soon...he didn't like to think what might happen. There was probably enough to be going on with to arrest the wife, if it hadn't been for the annoying fact that she had an alibi. Everyone he had spoken to swore that Patricia Wilcott had arrived with her husband after the preserves registration had finished, and had then been in the main Hall, helping to set up stalls for the whole time before the judging began. The Detective Inspector was sure that she must have popped out at some point but if so, no one was admitting it.

Margaret Mustard had been in the frame at the start, but DI Gordon had never seriously suspected her. He could quite imagine that she would make a scene at a committee meeting and bad mouth the man all over the village, but the plotting and stealth involved in poisoning her foe did not seem to fit with her personality.

The McScunnered chap had looked initially promising. He fitted the profile – DI Gordon instinctively felt that they were looking for someone with a grudge, financial or political – but he had thought the man would turn up during routine questioning. Perhaps he should have put more resources into hunting down the farmhouse after all.

He yawned again. Tomorrow evening. The Drummond Golf Club Desmond Wilcott Memorial Service and Portrait Unveiling.

Perhaps the breakthrough they needed would be there.

* * *

Everyone sat around the table, staring at Margaret. Patricia's face was deathly pale and still. Jessica couldn't believe she hadn't followed up on Margaret earlier. Why, when she had seen her behaving suspiciously in the park? When the woman had as good as told her the motive?

Margaret addressed her words to the MacNaughton. Maybe she found it easier that way. "Gillespie...I've been lying to you."

Jessica had never seen Gillespie MacNaughton look troubled. The most genial and relaxed of men normally, his face now betrayed his turmoil – lips set, eyebrows drawn together. He met Margaret's gaze unflinchingly and remained silent, waiting for her to go on.

"You have been ever so generous to me over the years Gillespie. You've let me use your finest malt in your favourite marmalade – the Castle Drummond Orange and Whisky. Dalkinchie and Drummond Craft Show prizewinner for eight years running! But I have something terrible to confess."

Jessica was getting impatient. It was clear that Margaret liked being the centre of attention, even now. A small exasperated sigh escaped her lips, but Patricia stayed her with a gentle look. Margaret took a deep breath and the next words came out in a tumble.

"Gillespie – my marmalade, I've been...I've been using a kit!"

This time Jessica didn't try to conceal her annoyance. "I don't really see what your preserving methods have to do with this? Can't you tell us when you poisoned it?"

"No, Jessica, this is relevant. Using a kit is against the Craft Show rules. The marmalade should have been entirely home made." Patricia was looking at Margaret through narrowed eyes. "But you have a good point. I would like to hear the rest, Margaret, the bit where you decided to murder my husband, and frame me for it."

A penny dropped for Jessica. She had seen marmalade making kits in the store, tins of prepared oranges. Margaret Mustard had been winning the top prize at Show for years with one of those?

"I...I never intended to blame you, Patricia. I'm not sure how that happened. I suppose everyone knows that you two didnae get on, and just assumed."

Jessica's mouth dropped open in shock. How could Margaret be so rude? Luckily Patricia was more than able to take care of herself. "Margaret, you can drop the act. You came to visit me on Monday. At first I thought it was strange, but then I chalked it up to your perennial nosiness! However I have just recently come into possession of some new information – " here she glanced at Jessica " – and I know for a fact that the vial of nicotine was planted on my mantelpiece after Sunday, but before Tuesday. Why on earth did you come round, if not to put it there to frame me?"

Margaret pulled her shoulders back and steadied her voice. "I visited, Patricia, because I believed that it was the kindest and most neighbourly thing to do under the circumstances. I am nothing if not community-minded! I had nothing to do with any nicotine and I don't know what you are referring to. I take any punishment that is coming to me, but I will not be accused of a crime that I did not commit."

Patricia opened her mouth, face flushed again, but before she could respond, the MacNaughton interjected.

"Hold on a minute here. Margaret, why do you think it wis your fault if you didnae handle the nicotine? Did you poison the marmalade by some other means?"

"Not intentionally!" Margaret crumpled again, her voice wavering. "It was an accident! The kit…the kit I used…well, it was out of date!"

Total silence followed this statement.

Then Patricia Wilcott burst out laughing.

"Out of date? Out of date marmalade? Oh, Margaret, if that could have got rid of Desmond, I would have tried it myself years ago." She checked herself, perhaps realising the inappropriateness of this joke under the circumstances. "You can put your mind at ease, Margaret. Pure nicotine killed Desmond, not some slightly dodgy oranges. I thought you would have heard? That's what I found in my living room, and that's what the test results showed."

"Aye, I did hear, but you know what the gossip around here is like – " Patricia's eyes met Jessica's briefly, and the latter quickly looked down, trying to suppress her smile " – I thought folk had just got the wrong end of the stick, because I was so, so sure that it was my kit that was bad. I was just so busy at the time, wee Dorothy was moving into the sheltered housing and I was helping with the flit, and we had all that fundraising for the church roof going on – I never got to the supermarket for a new kit and I thought it would be fine just this once. Oh Patricia. I am so sorry. Whatever you must think of me!"

"Not at all, Margaret…"

But Margaret was no longer listening, instead staring at the MacNaughton in contrition. "And I've thrown the whole lot out, Gillespie! I was so sure that the whole batch would be contaminated. Your favourite! All that marmalade!"

"And all that whisky," replied Gillespie, but he was smiling. It was just as well that he took it in good spirits because Margaret next moved on to the ruined dinner, and it took the promise of a takeaway pizza and convincing her that he was just as happy with jam on his toast in the morning before she would calm down. Patricia and Jessica left them to it, Jessica quite happy to be returned to Reenie's cottage to restore her dipping energy levels. Patricia was reflective on the journey home, but if she had any new suspicions, she didn't share them.

It was only later, as Jessica was dropping off the sleep, that something began niggling at her. Something someone had said – something she had forgotten.

What was it?

15

The Drive and the Golf Club

F riday morning brought pouring rain, and Jessica was glad that she had no need to go out. Unfortunately the afternoon brought high winds to go with the rain, and found Jessica and Magnus back at Drummond Primary School, this time reporting on an after-school Science and Technology club.

As charmed as Jessica was by the serious and focused children, and their patient explanations of the experiments they were running, her mind kept drifting back to the revelations of the previous day. With Margaret Mustard out of the picture – surely no-one could be that good an actress – who was still in the frame? She wished she had followed up the McScunnered leads after all. She had been half-hoping they would be able to do so again today, but the driving rain quickly removed any such notions. Even with his windscreen wipers 'at full lash' as he had described it, Magnus could barely make out twenty feet ahead – driving around and trying to spot Abbotsford under these conditions would have been fruitless. Jessica sighed. Still something nagged at the back of her mind; if only she could remember it things might be clearer.

"Miss! Are you watching? Miss?"

Jessica guiltily dragged her attention back to the present, where two adorable eight-year olds in white coats and plastic safety glasses were about to add vinegar to their baking soda 'volcano'. She would have to sort through her thoughts later. Right now it was time to act appropriately awestruck as the foaming lava overflowed the papier mache crater, and ran down the sides.

After the club had finished, Magnus drove Jessica to the bus stop where it had been agreed Ealisaid would pick her up, to maximise the time available for preparing the event. Jessica had brought her catering clothes with her. On the way, Jessica entertained him with the events of the day before.

Magnus slowed the car to a stop and turned to look at Jessica properly. "Oh my dear goodness. I cannot believe she really thought she had poisoned the marmalade wi' a tin o' foosty oranges. She really binned the lot?"

"The whole batch, she said! Protecting the citizens of Dalkinchie! I worked out later I had actually seen her do it, in one of the garbage bins in the park. She was behaving very oddly, and now I know why!"

"Protecting the citizens – ". These words and the thought of Margaret Mustard creeping furtively around the park set Magnus off again, laughing harder than ever. Jessica was glad he was no longer driving – but she couldn't help but join in with his hilarity. For a few moments they sat in the car, heavy rain drumming on the roof, laughing uncontrollably. Any time it looked as if they were about to stop, one of them would say something which started it all up again.

"Reports of a serious marmalade shortage in Dalkinchie

are coming through..." This was Magnus, mimicking a news reporter. Jessica chimed in with, "In the interests of safety, citizens are advised to consume NO preserves. That's no marmalades, jams or curds. In fact, to be on the safe side just eat DRY toast. DRY toast is the official advice."

Magnus next mimicked the high, wavering tone of a much older man. "Aye, I mind well the great marmalade drought – it started wi' the Castle Drummond Orange & Whisky. Once it wis abundant, then suddenly there were nae jars. Not a single jar in the whole of Dalkinchie or Drummond! Not one! Can you even imagine that, you young folks?"

Jessica continued to laugh but she was suddenly struck with a thought – followed by another. Two details that had been nagging at the back of her brain revealed themselves, and all at once, things fell into place.

* * *

Magnus had to get back to Balnaguise for evening milking. He left her at the bus shelter, after extracting reassurances that she would be just fine. Ealisaid was due along in a few minutes, and Jessica was confident that The Drummond Golf Club Desmond Wilcott Memorial Service and Portrait Unveiling was exactly where she needed to be heading.

With the rain drumming hard on the shelter's thin roof, she pulled out her cell phone and, glancing at it, realised she had missed a voicemail.

The message was patchy. Jessica wasn't sure if it was her signal or something to do with the phone, but she could only make out every other word. "Hi Jessica, I've having a bit *****bother, and I'll be *****straight to the *****. Just stay at the bus stop

194

in Drummond, I've got *****to pick you up and I will see you there. Stay at the bus stop!"

Frowning, Jessica tried to replay the message, but the phone died. Jessica sighed in exasperation. Looking up quickly, she realised that Magnus was already out of sight. Nothing else for it. She settled in to wait for her promised ride. At least there was a bus shelter, although it wasn't very effective against the diagonal rain.

A few long, damp minutes later she thought she detected a pricking of lights through the murky rainfall, then the distant sound of an engine above the thudding of the rain on the bus shelter roof and walls. A few more moments and it was definite. A car was coming towards her through the rain. Thank goodness! The rain was pounding so heavily that she couldn't make out the driver, but it was definitely slowing as it approached. The white car pulled up smoothly at the side of the road, and the passenger window rolled down.

"Miss Greer. I thought I would find you here. Ealisaid Robertson asked me to pick you up. I understand that you are headed to the Donaldson Cup Memorial service? Hop in, I will give you a lift."

Jessica had stepped out of the bus shelter as the car pulled up. The rain lashed hard against the hood of her raincoat. With her phone out of batteries, she had no means of contacting anyone, and it would look incredibly suspicious if she refused the offer now. It wasn't as if she could outrun him – he was in a car and she was on foot in the rain – and really, he could have no reason to think she suspected anything at all.

What other choice did she have?

She looked into Donald Donaldson's florid face. "Thanks. That would be great."

* * *

Jessica got into the car. As they drove, she tried to keep the conversation light and minimal, and completely off the top of Desmond Wilcott's murder. Instead, she filled the silence with non-stop chatter about the school science club, and how clever the children were. Donald Donaldson paid little attention, checking the road, looking in his side mirrors and saying nothing at all.

The car turned into a dark, tree lined road. On one side, flashes of green could be spotted between the trees. On the other, just more trees. The car slowed down, and finally came to a halt at the side of the road.

"Why have we stopped?"

"I think my brakes are a bit spongy in these floods, and I am concerned about one of my brake lights. Would you mind getting out and checking if it is working?"

Again, what choice did she have? Wordlessly, Jessica opened the passenger door and moved to the back of the car. The rain had perhaps lessened a little, but it was still pouring. Her senses were on high alert now, but true to his word, Donald Donaldson drove a little ways off, then applied the brakes. Both brake lights glowed red. Jessica gave a shaky thumbs up. She didn't trust the man, and was prepared to leap into the ditch if he did anything unpredictable – like, for instance, trying to reverse over her.

Instead, he exited the car which was still parked twenty yards or so from Jessica, and walked steadily towards her, swinging a golf club.

The man stood in front of her was still the slightly shambolic Donald Donaldson but with a new and menacing air. His pale grey suit was quickly turning dark with rain, and his hair was plastered to his face. Jessica didn't like the way this was going at all. Was it something she had said? Her words ran back through her head...she surely had not said anything revealing.

"I hear you have been chatting to Patricia. She was very interested in what you had to say about the trophy. I must say, Miss Greer, it would have been a lot better had you not interfered in things that do not concern you. At all!"

Jessica froze. He was close enough now that she could see the rain dripping from his nose.

"About what trophy?"

It was the worst thing she could have said. It was far too late to play the innocence card.

"Oh, I think you know. The Donaldson Cup trophy, of course! Founded by my very own Great-Grandfather and won, year after year, by my good friend Desmond Wilcott! Sitting on his mantelpiece right here in Drummond, a shining beacon of his golfing success!"

There was no mistaking the sarcastic emphasis Donald Donaldson had placed on the words 'good friend'.

"She says you found it empty on Sunday, and of course Patricia found some nicotine in it later that week, placed there by my good self on one of my many visits to check up on her. I think on that occasion I even took my wife. The two of them, chatting away in the kitchen – they had no idea what I was doing. The police were meant to find it and arrest her, of course, and would have if they weren't a bunch of useless incompetents. I told Patricia that you were probably mistaken, but she would have none of it."

"Of course, you are the only witness. It's just my word against yours – and if yours were silenced..."

There was no mistaking his intent. He raised the club to

strike. High speed possibilities flashed through Jessica's mind. She could try and reason with him, persuade him that no-one would believe whatever implausible excuse he had dreamed up for this scenario. She could promise that she would say she must have been mistaken. She could try screaming at the top of her voice.

Or she could run.

16

The Picture of Guilt

Jessica threw herself to the side and in a split second had squeezed between the trees and over the stone wall she had spotted on one side of the road. She had taken the flashes of green to be fields but now that she was running on it, it was unmistakably the beautifully maintained green velvet of a golf green.

There would be nobody playing in this downpour.

At first, the only direction that Jessica took was 'away' – from Donald Donaldson and his swinging club. As she ran, however, she tried to work out what she might be running towards. She risked a glance backwards – nothing. He had not followed her, no doubt realising that she could easily outrun him. He did have a far better knowledge of the golf course than she did, though, and the local geography. Who knew when she might be brought close to the roadside again, and where he might try to cut her off?

She tried to stay in the open area, and keep her direction consistent. It wouldn't do to run around in circles and exhaust herself. It was still raining; perhaps not quite as hard as it had earlier, but still hard enough to make visibility difficult.

And then – in the distance – surely that had to be the clubhouse? It was a long, white building which had clearly had multiple additions and extensions over the years. The roof was red tiled and peaked, the many windows were highly polished; the whole building exuded an air of class, sophistication and wealth that Jessica certainly did not reflect as she reached the front door, soaked and gasping for breath.

She ran inside. The first thing that she saw was a small sign at the bottom of a flight of stairs, stating that the 'Donaldson Cup and Wilcott memorial ceremony' would be taking place upstairs in the Donaldson room. More Donaldsons! There was no-one else in sight but she was sure she had caught sight of Ealisaid's old blue Beetle in the corner of the car park, although in her panicked dash she hadn't paused to check. Donald Donaldson was travelling by car, too, and she didn't know what route he could have taken. Could he be here already?

Jessica bolted up the stairs. The striped carpet was soft, and the sound of her running footsteps disappeared into the thick pile, giving her the eerie sense of lack of progress. Running without moving, just like in a nightmare. Would she be able to hear if he came after her? She looked back over her shoulder – nothing, for now.

The long, wide corridor was lined with portraits, gilt framed, mostly men, each with its own light source positioned directly above. Soon, Jessica thought, they would be joined by the murdered Desmond Wilcott.

Ahead were wide glass doors and through them – finally – Jessica could see a small gathering of people. Safety.

* * *

Bursting through the doors she finally began to feel her fear recede a little. At first she didn't recognise anyone in the room, but soon her eyes began to distinguish a few familiar faces. The room was long and rectangular, and Jessica had entered through doors on one short end. The long left side was completely taken up with large windows, and on the right there was a low platform stage set up with a microphone, a couple of chairs and, at one end, a covered easel. Four rectangular concrete pillars ran floor to ceiling at equally spaced intervals in the room, and in between them chairs were placed in rows facing the platform, with a small aisle in the middle.

And then – a rush of relief! – there was Ealisaid, at the far end of the room. She was smartly dressed with her green tartan apron tied over a long black skirt and white blouse, her usual outfit for evening outside catering gigs. She was presiding over a couple of long tables set up at the back, and as Jessica made her way towards her around the chairs, she looked up in concern. Jessica tried to steady herself and walk slowly across the carpet, but she was conscious of her messy, damp hair, dripping coat, and no doubt flushed face.

Behind her, the entrance doors opened again. This time, it was Patricia Wilcott who entered, closely followed by Detective Inspector Gordon and Special Constable Murdo Smith. Of course, thought Jessica, they would want to attend and see if there was anything to be found amongst the golf cronies. Golf. It had turned out to be the key to the whole thing, although she wasn't quite sure exactly why.

There was still no sign of Donald Donaldson, but now she realized Grant Mack was there too, no doubt in his capacity as local reporter. Jessica realized that she hadn't checked in with him since her illness – she would have to make time to speak to him later, and thank him for his kindness. Not right now though. There was a murderer to unmask.

First things first. She had promised to help Ealisaid, and help Ealisaid she would. It looked as if her friend had nearly finished setting out the food, and Jessica hurried up to her, issuing her apologies.

"Jessica! Don't worry, it's fine – but what on earth happened? Did you have to walk here? You are completely drookit! Do you have your black clothes? Here – I have your apron in this bag. You can go through there."

Jessica, still breathless, promised she would explain everything later. Grateful for the chance to change her clothes, she dodged into the back room, which as luck would have it led to a bathroom with a full length mirror and proper towels. By the time she emerged, kitted out in her all black catering gear, damp hair pulled back into as professional-looking a hairstyle as she could manage, the room had filled up and it was time to start milling around and handing out the drinks. Some people had started to take their seats. A man wearing a heavy medal around his neck was standing on the raised platform, talking to a young woman who was animatedly gesturing to the easel as she spoke. Jessica recognised Nicholas Pringle as he entered, and he nodded to her as he joined a small group and started chatting.

And then – there was Donald Donaldson. Jessica froze, but luckily Ealisaid was nearer to him as he entered, and he took the glass of wine she offered. He glanced around but Jessica was able to briefly dodge his line of sight behind one of the pillars.

At that moment someone took the last of the glasses on her

tray, and she was able to retreat to the back of the room to refill it. As she re-entered the crowd, people were being encouraged to sit down, with Murdo and DI Gordon at the end of the front row beside Patricia. Jessica really wished she had had the opportunity to speak to them, but it had not been possible while serving. Donald Donaldson also took a seat in the front row, across the aisle from Patricia. The seats filled rapidly and Jessica, following Ealisaid's lead, stood at the back. The short presentation was to be followed by the food, and more drinks.

The man with the medal kicked off proceedings with a short, suitably solemn speech. He introduced the young woman who, as Jessica had suspected, turned out to be the portrait artist. Together they unveiled the portrait on the easel to restrained applause from the audience. It was an excellent piece of work, capturing Desmond Wilcott well. Jessica felt it would look entirely appropriate in the Golf Club setting.

Following this, the man with the medal invited Donald Donaldson to the stage, to say a few words about his old friend and golf partner. Jessica quickly dodged behind the pillar again. The movement caught Ealisaid's eye, and she looked over curiously. Donald Donaldson began to speak. "Desmond Wilcott and I shared many a golf game over our long friendship. I was proud to call him one of my closest friends," he began.

Jessica's heart thumped. It was now or never. Once again she wished that she had had the opportunity to warn DI Gordon and Murdo, but there was no time for that now. She stepped out from behind the pillar.

"Mr Donaldson."

Donald Donaldson looked expectantly towards her, his eyes narrowing in shock as he recognised her.

"If the two of you were as close as you say, I was wondering why you poisoned him?"

"Miss Greer!"

Shocked faces swivelled to look at Jessica. Her courage nearly failed her, but she continued on regardless, her voice wavering. "You swapped the jars of marmalade. You must have stolen one from the Castle Drummond kitchen, and you swapped it out when you were registering your wife's entries. You also must have done it right front of me and Ealisaid, and we didn't even notice. You placed the poisoned jar into the competition, knowing that Desmond, as Head Judge, would taste it first."

"I...I..." Donald Donaldson stuttered. Then he regained some of his composure. "I am well known in this community, the owner of a respected, decades-old local family business, and a seasoned member of the Golf Club of many years standing. I do not think that anyone is going to listen to the ramblings of some young...*American lassie!*" He spat the last words out with venom.

"Actually, I am interested in what Miss Greer has to say. Please continue, Jessica." DI Gordon had stood up at the end of the row, and so now did Murdo. Jessica, aware that they now directly blocked the path between the stage and the exit doors, continued, this time speaking directly to the Detective Inspector.

"Donald Donaldson tried to attack me on the way here."

There was a sharp intake of breath around the room, and the low buzz of conversation started. Beside Jessica, Ealisaid looked at her friend in alarm and reaching across, squeezed her hand. Comforted by the support, Jessica continued. "He thought that I might pass on information about the planting of the nicotine vial. I knew it wasn't there on Sunday, you see, which meant that only a few people had access to Patricia's house to hide it. Process of elimination.

"He also accidentally told me that he had enjoyed some of Margaret Mustard's Orange and Whisky marmalade for breakfast this week. I didn't pay any attention to that, until I later found out that all the remaining jars had been destroyed. The only explanation was that Donald Donaldson had got his hands on a jar...and he had. He ate the one he'd swapped. The one that should have gone into the Show. We should have realized that it wasn't tampered with on the day - it popped when it was opened. He had prepared it in advance."

The buzz of conversation had increased to the point that DI Gordon had to intervene by standing and raising his hands. Having achieved silence, he addressed Donald Donaldson directly. "Mr Donaldson, you are going to have to come with us for further questioning."

Donald Donaldson looked around wildly. There was nowhere now for him to go, no escape to make. As well as Murdo and DI Gordon, a few Club officials had stood and moved closer to the edge of the stage, and, as Jessica now noticed, so had Grant Mack. Still Donald Donaldson's next move shocked everyone.

Moving across the stage, he kicked over the easel, causing the portrait to come crashing to the ground. The artist's hands flew to her face. Donald Donaldson picked up the portrait in two hands and began to smash it against the floor.

"He. Was. A. CHEAT!" he bellowed, punctuating each word with a crash. "A ball-dropper! In that last tournament, I saw him! The ball rolled from right under his trouser leg. My golf partner for years, the respected businessman and stalwart family man – he was nothing but a dirty hustler. The Donaldson Memorial Cup? Don't make me laugh! He never deserved it.

No integrity, no loyalty, and no respect for my family name!"

Sickened, Jessica looked away from the tantrum. Ealisaid put an arm around her shoulders. Donald Donaldson was manhandled from the stage and led from the room.

The audience looked at each other, unsure of how to react or what to do next. The portrait artist was kneeling down beside her work, examining the damage – which looked to be mostly to the frame. Patricia Wilcott, stood at the front, had turned and was scanning the crowd. Grant was making his way towards Jessica. As he reached her, Patricia's eyes met hers, her look of concern was wiped away, and she gave one single, composed nod.

17

A Few Weeks Later

"Down! Willow, down!"

The little dog struggled, mostly because of her furiously wagging tail, but finally she bent her front legs and moved from her sitting position to lie down on the grass, where she watched Reenie expectantly, tail still thumping.

"Look, Jessica, look! She's done it!" As soon as Reenie said this, Willow bounded over and barked excitedly, clearly delighted with herself and looking for her reward which she soon received. "Yes! Clever dog."

Jessica smiled at the sight. They were spending a relaxed Sunday afternoon in Patricia Wilcott's garden, along with a few carefully chosen guests. She followed Patricia into the kitchen, carrying a tray of empty bowls to refill with snacks. The party had turned into a huge success. It was a cloudy yet dry day, the rolling hills behind Drummond standing out green and lush against a slightly steely sky. If you knew where to look, Castle Drummond was just visible. Patricia had thrown open the glass doors that led to the garden and dotted around occasional tables with snacks.

Patricia leaned against the window frame for a moment and watched as her daughter Helen played with Evie outside. The little girl was a mini-me of her mother, sweet yet serious faces with silky curtains of long, straight dark hair parted in the middle. The child had a habit of sweeping hers back with her forearm as she played, and was right now engaged in chasing bubbles that her mom was blowing, lifted out of her reach in a sparking ribbon by a late summer breeze. As Jessica joined Patrica at the window, Evie insisted on taking her own turn blowing the bubbles and, as children tend to do, blew too hard for the first few tries, spraying the mixture everywhere but having no success at a properly formed bubble. Her mom patiently modelled the gentle way of coaxing the bubble from its plastic ring and the little girl, determined, blew softly, first of all producing one or two that immediately burst until finally a perfect translucent sphere rose from the stem of the wand, floating into the air just in front of Evie's delighted face.

The expression on Patricia's own face brought a distinct prickling of tears to Jessica's eyes. Gone was the tension that had been there since Jessica first met her. She now realised that it always had more to do with Helen's plight than it had with the death of her husband. As shocking as the circumstances had been, the end result was that Patricia had her family safely back in the U.K. where she could be close to them and see her little granddaughter grow up. Whether it was the lack of a censorious father-in-law or not, Jessica knew that Helen's ex-husband had suddenly become more accommodating, realising that it was better all round if his child had a good relationship with her mother and grandmother. Taking a job transfer, he planned to move back to the U.K. himself, so that he and Helen could take up the challenge of co-parenting while still moving ahead with their separate lives. While it was still early days, Patricia had been very positive about how the situation was looking.

As was Jessica. If everything had gone according to plan with Mike, they would have been moving in together right now and Jessica would be about to start her graduate degree in journalism. Instead, she already had two months experience of real community journalism, a firmer idea of her own skills, and a new life in a place that was fully becoming home.

Jessica carried the replenished snacks out to the garden, and placed them on the picnic table. People milled about, both inside and out. The early September day was pleasant, but the sky held that peculiarly Scottish luminescence and Jessica was sure that she could detect a slight hint of chill, the earliest signs of fall. She scanned the horizon, still thrilling at the rolling Perthshire hills and swathes of thick lush forest in the distance. As summer drew to its close, Jessica felt more deeply rooted, more part of the local rhythms. She couldn't wait to see the changing seasons and experience a whole year in Dalkinchie.

She turned and moved back towards the house, and experienced a moment of deja vu. Surely she had done this before? No – she had visited Patricia on a couple of occasions, but this was the first time she had spent any time in the garden. From this angle though, the house, the wide gable, the old tree looked oddly familiar.

Patricia joined her. "Are you OK Jessica? Can I get you another drink? You've been running around helping, as usual. Make sure you have a snack yourself!"

Jessica smiled. "I'm fine. I was just admiring your house. I don't think I had ever taken it in properly before. Is it old?"

"Older than the neighbouring ones," Patricia replied. "It

would have been the old farmhouse at one time. The farmer sold the land to developers, and they built the other houses in a similar style, although it's never quite the same of course. It is a lovely house, and I have had some happy times over the years. I hope to have quite a few more."

Jessica followed Patricia's line of sight. She was once again watching her daughter and granddaughter, now throwing a ball between them. It squeaked every time it landed on the ground, which it did often, making the little girl giggle.

"Helen would have been not much older than Evie when we first moved here. It was such a big move, from the other end of the country, and leaving behind friends and connections. Desmond got the job, so we did it. And I always loved the house, even although it needed a lot of work when we arrived. Whoever lived here before us had the most horrendous taste, clashing patterns and colours everywhere, and the whole place carpeted in the most putrid mustard yellow." Patricia smiled at the memory.

"We changed a lot. Desmond, he...he was never one to put up with anything he didn't like! To his credit, the whole place was done within a year. We changed the name, too. It had the original farm name when we moved in, what was it now, something beginning with A..."

Jessica looked at Patricia, eyes wide. She didn't need the confirmation, but it came anyway.

"Abbotsford, that was it. Abbotsford Farm."

Author's Note

Thank you for reading *Death in Dalkinchie*! It's the first full-length novel in a series which will span at least ten books. If you enjoyed it, you can pick up the prequel novella *Murder in Bloom* which covers Jessica's move to Dalkinchie and the first mystery she has to solve there. All you have to do is join my mailing list, where I send regular snippets about my writing life, news about book releases, and my Scots Dictionary Corner which introduces and explains some of the vocabulary my characters use.

I wrote the majority of *Death in Dalkinchie* over the summer of 2019. As I complete it, the first hints of autumn are detectable in the air, just as they are for Jessica in the final chapter. I do have a loose aim of either writing or publishing the Dalkinchie books during the season in which they are set. The next book will be a Christmas mystery, published in December of 2019. I start preparing for Christmas early, so it is a positive pleasure to already be writing about it.

All of the crafts described at the Show are real Scottish crafts. Personally I don't have any skills for lacemaking, weaving, knitting or woodcarving (although I wish I did!). I have many close friends who do have these skills and I have been lucky enough to watch them in action, and, in some cases, become the proud owner of their work. I don't have an Orkney chair though. It's on my wish-list!

Dalkinchie and Drummond are both fictional villages, and so therefore is Castle Drummond (although it is very closely based on castles I know well.) The real historic MacNaughton Clan seat is Dunderave Castle in Argyll.

The Howff in Dundee is a real graveyard, and you can wander through it (I have) just as Jessica and Murdo did. While there are archives in Dundee, the Dundee City Archives as I described them are fictional. I placed them roughly in the location of the famous D.C. Thomson headquarters. Whether or not you are trying to find out the identity of an anonymous letter-writer, I would always recommend Dundee for a visit. It's a wonderful city, and unlike Jessica, you should definitely make time for the V&A.

With all best wishes,

Carly R.

About the Author

Carly Reid is the author of the Dalkinchie Mystery series. She is an avid reader who has loved books and stories since childhood, her favourites being cozy mysteries and Golden Age crime. After a career working in all aspects of the book trade, Carly decided it was time to write her own stories. The Dalkinchie Mystery series is the result.

Carly lives in Scotland with her family, although not in Dalkinchie!

You can connect with me on:
- ⊕ http://www.carlyreid.com
- ⌗ http://fb.me/CarlyReidAuthor

Subscribe to my newsletter:
- ✉ https://dl.bookfunnel.com/y6jmzqmwxv

Also by Carly Reid

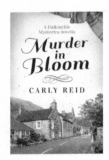

Murder in Bloom
A Dalkinchie Mysteries Novella
   A bad breakup, a new business...
      ...and a body in the cellar.

Jessica's future might be temporarily on hold, but her Aunt Reenie's could be over. Has Jessica got what it takes to solve the mystery before Reenie runs out of time?

When Jessica Greer comes to Scotland to help Aunt Reenie set up a new flower shop, she plans to get over her ex-boyfriend and find some comfort in her ancestral home - as well as help Reenie get ready for opening day. But when the local estate agent turns up dead in the new shop cellar, and the locals seems keen to pin the crime on an outsider, Jessica finds herself drawn in to the events, secrets and drama of a not-so-sleepy Scottish village.

Join my mailing list for a FREE digital copy of Murder in Bloom - a prequel novella that introduces Jessica as she solves her first mystery.

Yule Night Mystery - coming December 2019

Dalkinchie Mysteries Book 2

The perfect Scottish Christmas....if it wasn't for the body.

It's Jessica Greer's first Christmas in Dalkinchie and she is determined that everyone should have the celebration that they deserve, down to the last detail. When the Yule Night festivities end in a mysterious death, and it's looking like DI Gordon's Christmas will be more red tape than gift wrap - can Jessica solve the case in time to get everyone back home for their turkey dinner?

If you like twinkly lights, mince pies and murder, you'll love Yule Night Mystery.

Please note - this is not the final cover image